To Rick +
Molly W.

Spell of Appalachia
By Molly Wens

Cover Design: Joey Walnuts
Spell of Appalachia © August 2009 Molly Wens
eXcessica publishing
All rights reserved

To order additional copies of this book contact:
books@excessica.com

Chapter 1

The soul grows weary. There were some who never suffered the long-term effects of emotional exhaustion, those who have known little unhappiness. They were the lucky ones, traveling through life, blissfully unaware of tragedy and pain, of the horror that hides behind a brave smile. Those who knew that torment could only hope for something, for some place that would offer them solace and give rest to their disillusioned minds.

Such was the case for Onida Burke. She needed the quiet of this mountain retreat to calm the desperate craving that gnawed at what little remained of her dwindling spirit. The cavernous void that prevailed echoed with the screams of that inner voice that silently cried out for something unnamed. The aching chaos of it warred with the reverberant, whispery stillness of the mountains that surrounded her sanctuary.

She inhaled deeply of the earthy dampness that surrounded this place. Anticipation for what might be ahead held her immobile in silent vigil. A small crumb of hope barely enough to feed her flagging resolve, kept her there in suspense. She prayed for those precious moments that were needed to sustain her—a necessity almost as essential as taking a breath.

This current visit—this escape—had begun no differently from her many previous trips. To get to this moment, clinging to the slim hope of one twinkling instant in time, she had forced herself to endure the immeasurable torment of anticipation in the long hours of darkness. Another seemingly endless vigil spent as a sleepless night found her standing upon the balcony in the pre-dawn mists. This was where reality and magic seemed to couple and clash. In the convergence was sired a realm where dreams ruled and mystical creatures stirred within the veil of the fog.

The cabin—her retreat—was huge and sprawling, made of native pine logs and oak paneling. It was built directly into the side of the mountain, and its great balcony overlooked the forested valley that stretched downward to disappear in the mists. She came here as often as time would allow.

In this world, she was no longer Onida Burke. She was no longer pulled in every direction by editors, agents, and publishers. No one knew her in this place. There was no scandal, no clucking tongues and pity-filled glances. Here, she was safe from the past, if not the memories.

Her soul needed the solace and peace that only this place could offer. The many long and secluded weeks she had spent here throughout the past years were all that kept the dark nightmares at bay. The seemingly magical healing powers of this sanctuary had quickly become vital to her sanity.

Wrapped in the soft cotton quilt she had inherited from her grandmother, she listened to the muted sounds of her hazy valley below. The quilt's vibrant colors hailed the awakening day, urging it to burst forth into existence.

The resonance of her soul did not match the silvery music of the untouched morning; she was bone-weary and nearly crushed by the weight of what had happened almost two years before. That tiny ember of hope within, fading with each passing moment, threatened to suffocate as the awakening day approached.

She was lost in her musings when the air around her began to change. The sun had not yet brought in the filmy gray of dawn when an awareness crept along her spine and into her consciousness. It was a sensation that she had gratefully encountered on previous visits. She welcomed it now, voicing her relief in a faint sigh.

The hair at the top of her neck lifted, causing her skin to prickle. She tensed as a mockingbird trilled in the darkness. It was impossible to tell from which direction the bird called, so thick was the mist. This setting was becoming familiar, but it still never ceased to astonish her. Onida knew she was not alone.

He was suddenly there, soundlessly formed from the vapor that surrounded her. The power of his presence announced his silent passage into the physical plane. Before the first touch of his hands, the radiant heat emanating from his body warmed the back of her quilt. It was almost tangible in its intensity, this surreal energy that encompassed his presence.

Onida was afraid to move, fearing that the mere motion of her body would cause him to disappear as he had done so many times before. She knew it was him. No one else could invade her cognizance with such captivating urgency. It had to be him. Still, she dared not move.

As if by sorcery, the quilt lifted away from her shoulders and fell in a pool at her feet. The crisp morning air nipped at her through the thin white satin of her sleeveless nightgown. She shivered slightly, but soon became oblivious to the chill. It seemed an endless moment before there was actual physical contact. Was it really physical contact, though, when she could not be sure whether this was a living man, a phantom, or an invention of her lonely mind? When his hands finally settled upon the bare skin of her arms, his touch was cold as death and hot as the fires of hell. She responded with a rush of breath hissing through her parted lips.

The pain of the past months lay forgotten like the quilt at her feet. Her mangled soul ceased to ache as her body warmed under his touch. The two men lying in those graves weren't tormenting her at present. Raw guilt no longer devoured what was left of her spirit. She had ceased to care, if only for this moment. All that mattered now was this haunting apparition, the one who held his tense body just inches from her own, whose hands rested so deliberately upon her flesh.

He had been here before. He had always seemed like an invention conjured by her mind when her need was greatest. But his touch had grown so lifelike. Was he real or not? It was a question she had never been able to answer. These meetings had been so few and fleeting, but all that mattered at present was that he was here now.

Her body's need for him had become so great that there was no stopping it from melting under the heat of those amazing hands. She leaned back into him. A low moan escaped her lips as his arms slowly encircled her, his palms grazing her nipples through the thin cloth of her nightgown along the way. Again, there was a shiver working along her spine. Her need burned with the same fire as his touch.

He pulled her deeper into his embrace, the stubble on his face grazing the soft skin of her cheek. The pure potent essence of him intoxicated her senses; the smell of woodlands and rivers, of wind, rain, and morning dew.

The tip of his tongue traced the line of her jaw. Her knees began to buckle, and he supported her as if she weighed no more than the air from which he was formed. The sensation of his scalding flesh against her exposed back brought the obscure realization that somehow he had managed to remove her nightgown.

She was past wondering, though, and cared little about the "how."

He lifted her, carrying her to the bed inside the room off the balcony. As he laid her down, she caught her first glimpse of his luminous face. It appeared to glow with an extraordinary inner brilliance. His eyes burned with a passion that she knew must have been mirrored in her own face. She wanted to know him, his body, his heart, his mind.

His lips touched hers in a damnably fleeting kiss. Her mouth quivered, crying out for more. There was a challenging light in his shimmering eyes as he bent to offer a second kiss. This kiss was scorching, searing her very soul with its intensity.

He appeared to glide upward to hover over the bed before he descended to settle on top of her, the full weight of his body pinning her to the feather-packed mattress in delicious captivity. His hands roamed her body with the same frenzied hunger that she had only experienced in his arms.

His thumbs scraped her nipples and the flesh that surrounded them. Soon his mouth followed, adding fuel to the fire that he stoked so passionately. The flames curled in the pit of her belly and spread wildly throughout her being. This wraith, whose teeth so skillfully nipped at her breast, was her lifeline. She clutched his hair and arched against his mouth as moan after moan broke from her throat.

His mouth and hands wandered lower, exploring the pale skin of her rib cage and soft belly. Moist, hot kisses rained sweet torment upon her impassioned flesh. The fire only slowed in descent for a moment as he paused to savor her navel with his tongue.

His hands traced a path of flames along her hips as he resumed his downward quest. Her cry of pure pleasure pierced the stillness of the morning when his tongue found the cleft between her legs. He lifted her thighs, spreading them and pushing them up away from his head. His tongue, his lips, and his teeth worked together to create sensations that drove her to some primitive level deep within her subconscious, where only this tormenting pleasure existed.

So wrapped up was she in these supernatural sensations that she failed to realize the moment his mouth left her and his granite center found her. Her legs were about his ribs and her nails dug into the flesh of his back as he entered her, impaling her flesh in one powerful motion. His manhood was alive inside her, pulsing and pumping while driving her to the brink of a frantic state where only his body existed for her.

A desperate shriek burst into the pre-dawn air as the first wave of endless orgasm shook her. It was soon joined by his loud, feral growl as he joined her in climax. He drove into her harder and harder until finally, he collapsed over her, sated and emptied.

She remained immobile on the bed, all control over the muscles of her body lost to the complete fulfillment of his lovemaking; his unearthly, yet heavy, body panting on top of hers. Sapped of all strength, she could only yield to the power of the emotions that penetrated to her marrow. She felt a single tear escape her eye. He kissed it away, a tender gesture of endearment. Then his lips embraced hers, reaching to her very center. She prayed it would never end.

She voiced her disappointment in a moan as his lips left hers. He stood and looked at her in the first shadowy light of misty dawn that came in through the door. A burning smile crossed his lips—a smile that seemed to promise so much more.

Then he was gone, swallowed by the hungry mists of the mountain as they swirled over him. She sat clutching the soft cotton of the bed sheet against her breasts, watching as his body dissolved, the outline of him flying apart and dissipating into the surging fog.

"Don't go," she whispered.

Her shaky legs threatened to give way when she tossed the sheet aside to stand. It took all her strength to stumble out the balcony doors and into the clearing mists. He was nowhere to be found, just as always. All that remained was the fading song of a distant mocking bird.

The damp and chill of the dawn air finally drove her inside. She bent to retrieve the forsaken quilt along her way. If she had felt alone before, it was nothing compared to this acute hollowness that overpowered her now. A blackness settled on her soul that might have frightened her had she the strength to care.

She wrapped the quilt around her nude body and curled up in the center of the big feather bed. The cotton sheets still held his scent. She breathed deep of his fragrance. Dark emptiness tightened its grip on her. The woman knew that he would not return to her again this visit, and suddenly her refuge held no solace for her anymore; it was time to go home to try to face her life once again.

Chapter 2

It had happened again. He knew as soon as he woke up because every muscle in his body felt as if it had been stretched to its fullest. He knew because he awoke naked. His cock, slick and wet, still throbbed as if it had just been joyously buried in the body of a woman.

He was too old for wet dreams, although that would have been the most logical explanation. He had never been known to sleepwalk, but even though it was mainly a malady afflicting youngsters, it had been known to start in later years, given enough stress. He nearly laughed as the ludicrous notion of being abducted by aliens for breeding experiments crossed his mind. The press would have a field day if it ever got out that he, Liam Cannan, the CEO of Cannan Enterprises was entertaining such ideas. In truth he had no idea what had been happening to him.

It first started less than two years ago. He had awakened at dawn in this very same condition. He had memories of a dream, or that's what he had told himself at first, that it was an incredibly vivid dream. He normally did not remember the conjurings of his sleeping mind, but this one stuck in his memory; it was a dream that, in part or in whole, had been repeating these many months.

It was always the same woman. A woman he had never met or seen, at least not in the waking world. She had a beauty that was rare—chestnut hair that curled around her shoulders, and deep brown eyes that had fire behind them—a fire that could kill a man where he stood, or melt him into a blissful pool. Her skin was that of china, soft to the touch and the shade of fine paper.

Her body...he had seen her body in dream after dream. It was the body of a woman that men have desired for eons. Her breasts were full and round, with large, pointed nipples that stared her victims straight in the eye. Her rib cage made the perfect bridge from her magnificent breasts to her softly rounded stomach. Below her waist, she had an ass that called to him, an ass that screamed to be kneaded. Her legs were shapely and long. They met with the thinnest line of pubic hair. In his dreams he often had the occasion to see even more. Leave it to say this was a woman that he would have pursued to the ends of time in the real world, if only she existed.

All of the dreams took place in the same general location. One he had never seen while awake. It was a cabin in some backcountry, peaceful and secluded.

The dreams all started in different ways. There were times when Liam would see the woman in the cabin. Sometimes she would see him approach, other times not. But he would always approach. He could never stop himself from touching her. Sometimes she would be in the woods, walking, or lying on a blanket writing in a notebook. There were times he would find her in the stream nearby.

One thing the dreams all had in common was that he always wanted her. It was a want that went deeper than passion, deeper than sex. He wanted to become one with the woman. He wanted to know her and for her to know him, but for some reason, he never had a voice in the dream. Instead he used his body to try and communicate his desire. He would walk up behind her sometimes and gently stroke her shoulder or her face. She always seemed to feel his touch, even if she didn't acknowledge his presence.

Then there were the dreams wherein he would enter the darkened cabin and find her asleep in bed. At first he could never resist climbing into bed with her, to feel the heat of her body. He would enter her from behind or climb on top of her and ply her with kisses. As time went on and the dreams continued, he spent several of these visits standing at the foot of the bed, watching her sleep as she tossed and turned under the thin sheets.

But more often, Liam's passion for this woman was too strong not to take her body. She never seemed to protest. This last dream was different from the others. In this one, she seemed to be waiting for him. The way she had melted under his hands, it was as if she had been expecting him. The woman had given completely of herself. For a relationship that continued without dialogue, full acknowledgment, or even consciousness, it was the most intense bonding he had ever had with a woman.

There were times when they would make love for what seemed like hours, both giving in entirely to the other's desire. Other times, it was quick as a flash fire and twice as intense. Every time he felt her wrap herself around him he thought that it would break the charm and bring one or both of them to the full reality, whatever it was—but it never did.

Over the past six months, he had decided that these encounters had to be dreams. But they were so real. There had also been other forms of physical evidence such as scratches across his back, bruises he could not remember having when he had gone to bed. So, if it wasn't a dream, what was it? Had he lost his mind and been hunting rape victims? Was he missing time due to a magnetic field? Did he have a brain tumor and was living two separate lives, each only recognized during its existence, with the other only appearing to be a dream?

Who was this incredible woman? Why could he not find her if she was in the real world?

Chapter 3

Onida found herself on the plane, with a flight attendant standing over her, asking some inane question, while visions of his face came back to haunt her. His eyes, alight with mysterious flames, hovered just inches above her as his hand tenderly stroked her cheek. It suddenly occurred to her that he had never spoken to her. Had he no voice?

"Ms. Burke?" The voice seemed to come to her from a great distance and inch by inch she rose out of her reverie. She looked up to see the beaming woman who was serving drinks in the first-class cabin.

"I'm sorry?" Onida responded distractedly.

"You are the Onida Burke, aren't you?" the gushing woman asked. Before Nida could answer, the attendant went on. "Of course you are. I just love your work. I have every book you've ever written. I wish I had them all here right now so I could ask you to autograph every one."

Nida found the first shards of annoyance breaking at the edges of her patience. She forced a smile to her face and murmured something complimentary. "May I get a drink?" she added.

The blushing attendant rushed ahead to comply. The annoying little woman was still glistening with pure idolization.

"What will it be? Wine, beer—I know, champagne," the attendant cooed.

"Just vodka," Nida returned with a sudden urge to punch the happy little twit. "On the rocks," she added with a bogus smile.

She kept the ridiculous grin on her face until the attendant finally excused herself and moved to the next passenger.

Nida had finished her fourth drink by the time her plane finally touched down in Chicago. The weather on this early autumn day seemed to reflect the darkness of her soul. Finally, she thought, something matches me .

O'Hare airport was alive with activity as people rushed catching their flights or meeting loved ones. Nida paid them no mind as she headed for the exit, knowing her bags would be sent on later—she just wanted to get home. A limo, complete with her panic-stricken agent, was waiting for her. Nida fairly groaned when she saw the short, little man with more hair in his ears than on his head. He wore his ever-present bow-tie tightly cinched around his neck. It was something she had always found amusing, but lately her sense of humor had abandoned her.

She failed to listen to him as the black car carried them to her building. Her penthouse was at the top of twenty-six stories, and she felt like jumping out the window by the time Robert Goldman had walked her to the front door. He had been nagging at her all the way from the airport, like an irritating insect buzzing in her ear. The minute she was in her apartment, she rudely slammed the door in his face.

Nida stood in the entranceway, staring about the apartment. It seemed so cold, so empty. Nothing had changed since before that day, and yet this place was not the same. She clenched her fists and ground her knuckles into her eyes as a fresh onslaught of guilt and horror overtook her. Death, cruel and unyielding, had visited here, staining her life with its poison. It would never go away.

The visions of the voiceless, nameless lover were replaced by another memory. This memory was death. Eyes, frozen in horror and time, came out of the shadows to haunt her. She dared not look into them, as they most certainly would mean her end. For the first time in her life she began to crumble. Her legs would no longer support her; her heart could no longer bear the pain. Her mind closed in on itself as a single ghastly shriek shredded the afternoon. Her knees buckled. All light faded into oblivion.

* * * *

Somewhere, hundreds of miles away, a man poring over account books suddenly felt a bitter nip at the edge of his consciousness. He was not sure what it was that he was feeling, but he had the distinct impression that someone had just stepped on his grave. Something akin to dread drifted over him. He couldn't put his finger on anything specific, but he unexpectedly thought of the woman from his dreams. He shook his head, cursing himself for a fool, but still, he found it difficult to focus on his work.

* * * *

The next evening Nida woke to find herself in unfamiliar surroundings. A man in a white coat was standing over what passed for a bed under her, grinning like a fool. "We were a little worried about you, Ms. Burke. Glad to see your eyes open."

Nida looked around in astonishment. "Where am I?"

The man in white went on to explain, as if reading her thoughts, "Your housekeeper found you unconscious on your apartment floor. I'm Dr. White. I've been taking care of you. It's nothing too serious. I believe you're suffering from exhaustion."

The man's eyes, though kind, weren't filled with fire. Thankfully, neither were they filled with death. She tried to focus on what he was saying but it was damnably strenuous. She listened as the man went on.

"I know it's a little confusing. You've been asleep for thirty-three hours. It will be a bit difficult to focus for awhile. As I've said, you are suffering from exhaustion. There wasn't any next of kin that we could locate so we spoke with your agent, I hope you don't mind. He says that you have a cabin retreat in the Smokies that you can go to for rest. That's what I want you to do, rest."

Nida shook her head. "I just got back from there. I have work to do."

Dr. White's eyes lost their kindness and became hard. He leaned in closer, fixing her with a stern look that would have done her mother justice, once upon a time.

"You need rest," the man insisted. "This could be very serious. I understand that you've been under some strain."

Nida flinched at those words. Somehow, having someone speak to her of what she was responsible for, made her feel defiled.

"I have work."

"You won't have work if you're dead. You must rest. Your agent has arranged for a nurse to meet you at your cabin. You will need someone to take care of you."

At that moment Bobby Goldman waltzed into her room. The man's timing was impeccable.

"Nida, my dear, you had me worried. I'm pleased to see you awake. I was near scared to death when that Ukrainian woman of yours called me. She was so upset that I had a devil of a time trying to understand what she was saying. Feeling better?"

"As opposed to what?" Nida answered in a sour tone. "Dr. Killjoy here is under the impression that I'm going to the hideaway. He even says that you got me a nurse. Well, forget it. I have too much work to do, as you so aptly pointed out yesterday—or the day before or whatever..."

Goldman dismissed the doctor with a wave of his hand, assuring him that Nida would indeed be leaving town. He perched on the edge of her bed and took her hand.

"Nida, I love you," he said with sincerity. "Not just as a client, but I think of you as a member of my own family. I didn't realize...didn't pay attention to how ill you were when you got off that plane. I should have known after all you've been through."

Again, Nida flinched. She pulled her hand free and crossed her arms over her chest.

"That's enough," was all she said.

He patted her leg, saying, "Don't worry. You don't have to talk about it. But you do have to rest. The manuscript can wait. You have to take care of yourself. Go back to the cabin, rest; let the woman take care of you. Come back in a few weeks with your batteries recharged and your motor running." He kissed her cheek as he stood to leave. "Your bags are already packed. You may as well go. You can't work like this. Go."

After he left, Nida was alone with her thoughts and the eyes of the dead that flashed into her memory. She shook her head to dispel the vision, but it was only replaced by another—this vision had eyes that burned.

"All right," she yelled at the closed door. "Sign my ass out, then!"

She was going back to her beloved mountain. She was going back to him...at least that's what she hoped.

It was for that reason that she found herself, once again, on an airplane. Apprehension mingled with something else to make her wish she could just keep flying until the world disappeared behind her and there was nothing left but deep, dark space. She didn't want to be in Chicago—she was afraid of returning to eastern Tennessee.

So she drank—heavily. She drank so much that if it had not been for the lap belt holding her in her seat, she would have spilled out onto the floor of the jet that was touching down on the runway at Knoxville. When it was time to get out of her seat she listed slightly, one of her fellow passengers catching her before she could fall face first into the aisle. She mumbled her thanks and stumbled toward the exit without looking up.

Chapter 4

It was a moment frozen in time. Fate had decreed that his small company jet was undergoing an overhaul at just the right time to put him on this commercial airliner. Liam had not flown commercially in years and yet, there he was on that plane, on that day.

The minute his hands seized the stumbling woman a shock wave shot through him, as if some electrical force had stung him. Then he saw her face—the face of the woman from his dreams, inconceivable though it was. This was the woman who occupied his every thought, the reason he was about to lose his biggest account, and the reason he didn't care about it.

She didn't see him as he grabbed her arms, nor did she look up to find out who was touching her. The incoherent words she had muttered were in the voice he remembered, but the voice was barren, without the musical quality that resonated through his soul. Her face, so beautiful and golden in his dreams, was pallid, almost colorless. Her eyes were dilated and glazed as if she had been drugged.

The shock of seeing her had him in a stupor, staring after her in a daze. She had disappeared into the departing crowd of passengers before he snapped out of his narcosis to run after her. The aisle of the aircraft was too narrow and too crowded, forcing him to fight his way to the exit—but she was gone.

Liam suppressed the bellow of rage and frustration that had nearly exploded from his chest. Standing in the airport terminal, he forced his mind to work, to think about what had just happened. It dawned on him that something was wrong, something about the woman wasn't normal. Desperation rising in his heart, he realized that she had looked ill. He stood in the middle of the terminal as panic nearly overtook him. There was the gut-wrenching feeling that time was running out.

* * * *

Onida found herself in an airport shuttle, sitting next to a cheerful yet domineering woman in her mid-fifties. Delma Clack, she had called herself, was a nurse by trade and motherly by nature. She was a small woman with graying red hair, pale weathered skin and a kind, round face. Bobby had outdone himself this time. Nida realized she wouldn't be able to get a thing done with this mother hen around. Steeling herself to the notion, she sat quietly as the car pulled up the long drive to her sanctuary.

She stumbled once again and nearly fell in a valiant attempt to navigate the stairs leading to the front porch of her retreat. Delma Clack was quickly behind her, supporting her weight and rattling on about the evils of alcohol. With a mighty shove from the capable nurse, the two women were on the expansive porch of the cabin.

"My, what a beautiful place this is," the nurse said in what Nida had come to recognize as the local inflection. "We're going to get a lot of rest here, aren't we?"

"Who's 'we'?" Nida thought morosely as she fumbled for her keys. She spilled her purse onto the wooden planks and nearly shrieked in frustration.

Plopping herself down on the padded rocker to the left of the door, she turned to the nurse, saying, "You'd better go on without me, Mrs. Clack. I'll only slow you down."

It was a feeble attempt at humor at best and the nurse was not amused. She retrieved the forsaken articles off the wooden floor, found the keys and deftly opened the door.

"I told you to call me Delma, or Del, like most people do. Now, I promised that nervous agent of yours that you would get some rest, and that's exactly what you'll get."

Del grabbed Nida by the arm and pulled with a strength that belied her diminutive frame, effectively moving her inside. "Up those stairs yonder, and into bed. No arguments."

Nida only had enough strength to comply. She was woozy and exhausted and her bed was a welcoming beacon. After some minutes of stumbling around, she finally managed to get her clothes off. Putting on a pair of sweats and tee shirt from the cedar bureau proved to be even more challenging when her feet got tangled and she hit the floor.

Her sleep was troubled, though, plagued with the specter of deep, green, blazing eyes set in a face so masculine and rugged as to be illogical. She could smell him on her bed sheets still. The fragrance of him filled her dreams with all manner of delicious, agonizing memories. She awoke with her hair matted to her sweaty face. Del was standing over her with a knowing light in her eyes.

"Man trouble, I see," the nurse said with a shrewd nod. "Always comes down to that, doesn't it?"

"I don't know what you're talking about," Nida mumbled as she pushed her hair back from her face.

"You were talking in your sleep. You said something about someone named Mike and then you were talking about a phantom. You were begging him not to go."

Nida wished she could choke the older woman. Instead she blushed and pulled the old quilt over her head.

* * * *

On a long highway, driving through the Smoky Mountains, Liam was trying to break the land speed record. He had to hurry. He had to finish with this client, hopefully save the account and then set about the task of finding the image from his dreams. He scarcely noticed the beauty of the early autumn-kissed hills surrounding him. It was getting late. Liam would miss this appointment and his business would go under. But the thin, ashen woman would not get out of his head. He mashed his foot down a little harder on the gas pedal.

Cresting the next rise, he saw the valley below. At the bottom a misty fog gathered, turning the scene somewhat surreal. The sun—already low in the sky—cast strange shadows across the road. He came to the realization that all this was obscurely familiar. Her troubled eyes flashed into his vision and he nearly lost control of the rental car.

All the while his own voice bellowed in his head: She's real, dear God, she's real!

Chapter 5

For the next two days, Nida was plagued with more fitful dreams. They were a mixture of ecstasy and despair, with the eyes of a preternatural being—so filled with passion and searing heat—that kept mutating into the cold dead eyes of the man that had once been so much a part of her life. Death, it seemed, was reaching out to her.

She had taken to walking through the wilderness that surrounded her mountain home at all hours of the day and night. She was nearly catatonic, wandering much the way of the nighttime mists that meandered through the trees.

Nida found several areas on her land where she had experienced his presence, hoping that he would come to her there, but it seemed so hopeless. The hours she spent waiting only left her empty, the time wasted chasing a ghost that she believed would never come. It was still fairly early the second morning when she heard a mockingbird was singing nearby. That was the sound Nida knew would signal his arrival. She thought she felt his presence under a giant oak, but turned to find only the empty mists that swirled around her.

Her shoulders slumped in defeat, her head hanging low as misery began to feast again. The damnable bird was singing louder, as if scoffing at her. She sat upon a log, allowing the pain to wash over her until she felt something. It was a touch, soft as a butterfly's wing and as hot as a burning ember.

"You're here," Nida whispered, not daring to turn around again.

He did not speak, only touched. The hand on her shoulder reached up to caress the curve of her cheek, drawing a soft sigh from her lips. She wanted to fall back against him, to feel the hard heat of his body surrounding her, but stayed motionless, allowing him to come to her.

That was just what he did. Moving slowly, he stepped around to face her. His eyes, so bright and green, burned into her soul. She was mesmerized, unable to think or react. Nida could only sit in the prison of his gaze, trapped by the fire that burned behind his eyes.

She felt herself pulled to her feet. His hands were on her arms, his mouth hovering just inches from her own. He was moving closer, slowly inclining his head, his eyes never leaving hers. She licked her lips, her breath catching in her throat as she prepared to accept his kiss.

She had no clue what had happened. Did she blink? As quickly as he had arrived, he was gone, disappearing as if he had never been there. She could still feel the heat of his hands on her arms, still smell his fragrance that lingered in the damp air. With him went the mockingbird, its song dissipating amongst the sounds of the forest. She was alone again.

"No," she cried, her frustration sending the birds in the trees into startled flight.

Spinning around, all she found were the scattering mists and the undergrowth of the woods. The world around her fell into hushed emptiness. Not even the small animals of the forest stirred, leaving her alone with her disappointment.

Nida felt cold inside. She wondered if she would ever feel real warmth again. Then she wondered if it really mattered and if it wouldn't be better to just give up. Somehow, the idea of closing her eyes and never opening them again had more appeal than the emptiness of this life.

Del maintained vigilance over her charge, clucking her tongue in concern at the woman's seemingly troubled soul. She didn't know what kind of misfortune had befallen this poor creature, but she felt fiercely protective of her. Nida needed her, that much was certain. The nurse determined to do her best to save this child.

On the third day Nida managed to get out of bed near dawn, her body stiff and leaden, her favorite time of day in her refuge. As she had done so many times before, she wrapped herself weakly in Grandma's quilt and stepped onto the balcony. Looking over the edge, she viewed the long drop down the hillside to the valley floor. It was a compelling scene below her. She thought that if she could fly off this balcony and turn into a bird, she could fly away forever, leaving all this pain behind.

Nida was leaning too far to be safe, she knew, but she couldn't seem to pull herself back. The fragrance of the woods, the soft chill of the air and the sweet song of a mockingbird in the quiet of the hour seemed to beckon to her. She had the sensation of floating.

Then there was another fragrance, the scent of him in the air. Losing her balance, fear started to climb into her throat as she tried to untangle her hands from the heavy quilt. She felt the railing pressing across her thighs when she started to go over. Someone caught her from behind and pulled her back. A whimper of relief spilled from her lips when she felt the heat of the person behind her. She turned to look into his face only to discover she was alone.

For the first time since her childhood Onida dropped her head and wept out of self-pity. The loneliness nearly swallowed her whole.

With one hand on the doorknob of Nida's room Del doubted whether she should intrude on the other woman's privacy. She thought that she had never heard such a grievous sound as that of Nida's sobs. Something had wounded this woman deeply, and, Del thought, the girl was too young to bear such pain.

* * * *

True fear was replaced by a rush of fury as the ringing noise brought him to full wakefulness. Liam threw back the covers and snatched the receiver of the offending phone out of the cradle. "What is it?" he fairly howled.

"Mr. Cannan?" came the tentative voice at the other end. Liam winced. It was his personal secretary and he knew something must be wrong for her to wake him at this ungodly hour.

"What is it?" he snapped again, just a bit too harshly.

"Sir, I'm sorry to call at this hour but there's been a terrible accident. There's a fire at the Chicago plant. It's bad. CNN is showing it right now. The whole thing's in flames. Do you want me to meet you in Chicago?"

"No," he bellowed.

He just couldn't leave yet. So what if a third of his young company's assets were going up in smoke. He was close and needed more time. Rubbing viciously at his forehead, he knew he was already in too much trouble, though. Obligation weighed heavily on him, with hundreds of people depending on him for their livelihoods. There was no choice, he had to leave. Frustration and something related to grief began to well in his chest, making it difficult to breathe.

"Yes," he recanted. "Take the first flight out. I'll...I'll get there as soon as I can."

With that he slammed the phone down and bolted to his feet. Snatching up the remote control to the hotel room TV, he tuned to CNN and saw all hell breaking loose.

"Damn!" he yelled into the early morning darkness, tossing the remote onto the bed.

The plant would be a total loss. How many lives would be lost? How many families would suffer because of this? He didn't bother to shower or shave but quickly dressed by the electronic light of the TV. In three fast strides he crossed the room and flung open the drapes.

The scene outside stopped him in his tracks. The misty, ethereal fog that gathered around the hills surrounding the city brought back to mind the dream he was having before Mary had so rudely intruded with her phone call. The unknown woman had been standing in front of him, slumped over a precipice that threatened to swallow her. He had seized her just before she went over, could still feel her arms in the palms of his hands. She had seemed so weak and frail, almost broken. What had happened to her? The sound of her sobs had echoed through his mind as he awoke.

"Damn!" he yelled again and turned to pack.

* * * *

"How're you feeling today?" Del asked Onida. The nurse took her pulse as Nida sat at the breakfast table.

Nurse Clack was eyeing her with an intensity that made Nida more than a little uncomfortable.

"Like I need a cup of coffee."

"No coffee for you. Caffeine will only hinder your recovery. You need rest, and stimulants won't help you with that," Del said, releasing Nida's wrist with a gentle pat as she set a steaming cup of cocoa in front of her.

"Well," Nida said with a rueful smile, "if I have to give up my morning coffee, I can't think of a better replacement than chocolate."

"I feel the same way." Del gave her an amiable wink. "I'm told you like strawberries."

Nida was almost thrilled when her nurse handed her a plate of fresh fruit complete with the luscious berries.

"However on earth did you get these this time of year?"

"I have my ways," Delma replied while she set about tidying up the kitchen as Nida nibbled half-heartedly at her breakfast. "You'll never regain your strength if you don't eat, honey."

"I'm sorry. I just don't have much of an appetite."

Nida watched the other woman as she poured herself a cup of tea then took the seat on the other side of the table.

"I don't mean to pry but maybe if you tell someone what's got you so troubled it will help. I heard you this morning, crying as if the world was coming to an end."

Del watched her young charge as the emotions played across her face. She sipped her tea and chose her next words carefully. She waited for some sign from Nida.

"I'm sorry if I woke you."

"You didn't. I'm an early riser. What's eating at ya, honey?"

Nida was quiet for a moment before raising her eyes to answer, "I'm losing my mind."

Her voice was flat and emotionless. It sounded nothing like what was happening inside her mind.

"How do you mean?"

Nida felt her lacerated strength dwindle further. How could she tell this woman what had been happening to her?

Del didn't let the woman's silence dissuade her. She couldn't help her if she didn't know what was causing this illness.

"Well," she said, "are you hearing voices? Are you seeing things? Are you having panic attacks? What?"

"Yes," was all Nida could manage.

She didn't know this woman, but she suddenly wanted to unburden herself. She rarely spoke of personal matters, even to her friends. She never felt close enough to trust them, and she had no family left. She was tired, more tired than she had ever been, as if she were carrying a ton of weight in her arms and there was nowhere to put it down.

"Voices, hallucinations, and panic attacks? Lordy, girl, no wonder you're stymied. Perhaps you better tell me what you're seeing and hearing."

"It's nothing, really," Nida said with a thin smile. "I just have these strange dreams."

She was gazing out the window as she spoke, and Del turned to see what she was looking at. But there was nothing there except the majestic Smokies.

"What kind of dreams?" the nurse asked as she turned back to Nida.

"I'm not sure you can even call them dreams. In my apartment in Chicago I can't close my eyes without reliving the experiences I have here or the horror that happened there. And what happens to me here is just too weird to put into words."

Nida turned to look at her new confidante with uncertain eyes.

Del's heart went out to this poor, wounded creature. "I can see that you are certainly disturbed by something. Can you tell me about it?"

"If I do you really will think I'm crazy."

"Hush now, child. I'll think no such thing."

"I...lord, I don't even know where to start. What did Bobby tell you?"

"You mean that neurotic agent-fella of yours? Not much. Said you were suffering from exhaustion and stress. He didn't elaborate."

Nida was glad that Bobby could keep his mouth shut, but it might have been easier if he had said something about what had happened that day in her apartment. She closed her eyes against the fresh onslaught of memories that charged into her head, her hand trembling as she brought it to her throbbing temple.

"A bad thing happened almost two years ago."

It was difficult for Nida to start the speech but soon it tumbled out like a confession. She told of her fiancé, Tom, a man that she had been seeing for three years. They had become engaged but had not gotten around to setting the date. At one point she began to see changes in him—little ones, at first. He had become secretive and evasive when she asked him what was happening. He began losing weight and had become moody. There were times when he would rant at her over the most inconsequential things; even times when she feared for her safety around him.

Finally, her agent and loyal friend, Bobby Goldman, had covertly hired a private investigator to follow the man. It was then that his ugly secrets were made known. Drugs. Cocaine, crack, heroin, ecstasy. He was using and he was dealing. Bobby nearly had a stroke knowing the whole thing could have been disastrous for her career. When she was told about it she went straight away to his apartment to confront her fiancé, believing that if she got him some help then he would be all right.

That's when she discovered his other secret. He had a girl with him, no more than a child, barely eighteen, and a prostitute. The girl was bound and gagged, and he was engaged in what can only be described as torture. Nida was revolted, the bile rising in her throat as he tried, unsuccessfully, to lie about what was going on. She demanded that the girl be released, screaming terrible things at him as the prostitute escaped into the night. Proclaiming an end to the relationship, Nida hurled the diamond ring in his face.

Nida didn't look back or even bother to close the door as she ran out of the apartment. He was begging her not to leave him, as she ran, and vowing that he would make her sorry. Nida heard him screaming into the night that she would pay.

She had refused to see him after that. No matter what means he tried to use, he was unable to reach her. The man simply would not accept that Nida meant to have nothing more to do with him.

A couple of weeks later there was a banquet that she was supposed to attend. It was some big deal that Bobby had set up to gain her work more exposure. She had called an old and dear friend, Mike Jones, to escort her. He was a wonderful man with a big heart. Despite herself, she had even had a good time.

Her friend took her home at the end of the evening and walked her to the apartment. They found her apartment door open, and there was the faint wail of a siren in the distance, getting louder. They stepped into the place to find that it had been completely ransacked. She had to pick her way through the mess to try to get the phone. It was in the living room that she saw him. He was lying in wait for the two of them. In his hand was a gleaming revolver and on his face was a sinister smile.

Nida heard a scream, surprised to discover it was her own, and the report of the weapon that opened Mike's chest, blood splattering all over her face and clothing. Everything had moved in slow motion as she watched her dear friend drop to the floor, inch by inch, his eyes open, cold, already dead. Those eyes seemed to plead with her for understanding as Tom closed the distance between them in two strides.

Tom had seized her hand, laughing maniacally as he forced her fingers around the butt of the gun. He closed his own fingers over hers and laughed again as she struggled to get free. Then the barrel was under his chin. His eyes, the deranged eyes of a demon, bore into hers as he squeezed the trigger. Blood and tissue splattered onto her face and the smell of gunpowder filled the air. The report had been deafening.

When the cops burst in and found her standing with a gun in her hand, shrieking over the bodies, they felt the scene was too convenient. She became a suspect. The investigation dragged on for months.

The scandal had been terrible: famous author kills perverted junky lover and new boyfriend. Finally, the coroner declared the deaths to be a murder/suicide and it all died down, but her life had been irreparably damaged. There was not a moment of peace for her as those dead eyes continued to haunt her.

After the long disclosure was finished, Nida slumped in her chair. She was utterly depleted. It felt good to finally talk about the terrible period in her life. It felt good to get off her chest just how devastating it had been. She had loved Tom. She had seen her future in him, had believed in him. But he had been nothing like the man she thought he was. He had betrayed her on so many levels.

A tireless and unrelenting guilt continued to plague her every waking moment about what had happened to her best friend that night. The loss nearly choked the breath out of her every time she thought about him. Logically, she knew that there was nothing she could have done differently, but her heart just wouldn't let her be—now she felt as if she could no longer trust her own judgment.

Del let her rest a minute before speaking, feeling the other woman's pain as acutely as if it were her own. Eventually, she reached across the table to touch Nida's hand.

"You have been through a lot, honey," she said. "I know your trials have been great. We'll get you through this, you'll see. The good Lord never gives you more than you can handle."

Del stood and collected the dirty dishes from the table. Curiosity got the better of her and she just had to ask, "What's this phantom that you talked about in your sleep?"

Nida was dumfounded. She looked at the nurse in shock. Del reached over to pat her hand again.

"You talk in your sleep, remember?"

"Oh, yeah," Nida replied feebly. "That's the part that makes me think I'm losing my mind."

Del waited patiently for Nida to continue.

Onida sighed deeply. Once again she turned her head to stare out the window. In the distance, a fat black bear ambled between the trees.

"I don't even know how to talk about this," she began. "I bought this place a little over three years ago from an old woman who said she and her husband had built it together. She called it their cozy love-nest. She told me how much happiness the two had found here and said there was magic on this mountain. Well, there's something on this mountain, all right. I think it's a ghost."

When Nida stopped, Del pressed her further. "Go on, honey. Have you been seeing ghosts?"

Nida snorted. How could she tell this woman what she had experienced?

"I've been seeing something, or rather, someone."

"What do you mean?" the older woman asked, keeping a keen eye on her.

"I don't know how to explain it. Sometimes, when I'm sleeping, I feel as if someone is watching me. I open my eyes but there's no one there. Other times on my balcony, I can feel someone standing behind me. Sometimes he touches me." Nida stopped, knowing how preposterous it all sounded.

"This thing, this person, is in your bedroom?"

"Yes. I think so. And sometimes out in the woods. I don't know. It always seems so surreal. It's like everything is disconnected, like it's not really me that's experiencing it. But when it's over I..."

"Yes?"

"I don't know. I must be losing my mind."

"Are you sure it ain't some mountain man stalking you?" Del's face bore an expression of alarm.

"It's nothing like that," Nida assured her. "It's not really real. Do you know what I mean?"

"I'm not sure I do, but you've just told me that a strange man has been sneaking into your bedroom at night and you don't seem to be concerned."

Onida nearly laughed. If Delma Clack only knew what had really been going on.

"It's not at night. It's always at dawn. He's there and then he disappears." Nida stopped for a moment. She raised her eyes to Del's, fixing her with a profound gaze. "All I know is that when he's there I feel as if nothing can harm me, and when he's gone I want to die."

"At dawn, you say..." Del's expression changed. "Was he in your room this morning?"

"Yes, I think so. I almost fell off the balcony and someone caught me. I can't explain it but it seems like he's been hovering nearby since I got here. Like he's just beyond my vision, but now it feels like he's not here anymore."

"You almost fell off...Dear Lord, honey. Are you all right?"

Del's weathered face bore such dismay that Onida felt herself warming to the woman. Despite herself she knew that she had found a friend. There was something comforting in this person that was rare in others.

"Maybe," Nida sighed, "it's all just an illusion, and I really am losing my mind. Maybe it's just wishful thinking. You know, it's probably just my writer's imagination carrying me away."

"Maybe, maybe not." Delma voiced cryptically. "What that old woman said to you was true—there is magic in these here mountains. Indians knew it. They pray and live with nature up here. The people below are always telling stories about the mysterious goings-on in the higher elevations. 'Course they don't understand the mountain folk and that's probably the reason for their suspicions, but I've always felt that there was some truth to it. Who knows? Maybe this man of yours is real."

Del stopped for a moment. "Sometimes," she continued, watching her young charge, "when we are at our loneliest, someone comes to us, as if summoned by our troubled souls. Maybe that's what this is. Your spirit is crying out, and his is answering."

Onida took time to digest this, excusing herself from the kitchen and wandering out to the front porch. The morning was growing gray, and she was feeling even more dismally alone. Was Del right? Was there really magic in these mountains? If so, was it magic that brought this man to her? She couldn't understand how it could happen. The heroines from her novels were always so sure of themselves, but Nida only felt uncertainty. He had to be a figment of her imagination. This man couldn't really exist. With that thought, her flagging spirits dipped even lower. She stared thoughtlessly into the misty trees.

Chapter 6

Liam stood at the command post that was overseeing the furious action. It seemed as if hundreds of men and women in emergency clothes and equipment were scurrying all over the inferno that was threatening to be his ruin. Six people had died, twelve had been carted off to the hospitals and ten more were still missing. The entire plant, which encompassed more than two city blocks, was aflame. So many people had been lost. And the entire building was totaled.

Cannan Enterprises, Inc. was not likely to stand such a loss, and more than just these people here would lose their livelihoods. He rubbed his forehead as the soot-covered plant manager informed him that the last shipment of product had not yet left the building. Everything had gone up in that noxious cloud of black smoke that turned the morning sky to night.

With each passing hour more bad news found him. Jake Olsen had been found. His boots were the only way to identify his charred remains. Grace Johnson was found crushed to death under a fallen chunk of concrete. The death toll rose and, outside the gates, family members gathered to find out about their loved ones. From time to time there was another explosion from the remains of the building that would send burning debris and sparks showering down on the fire crews.

It took two days to bring the fire under control, and another two days to put it out completely. In the end there was nothing left except for a scorched skeleton of a building and charred rubble. The crowds outside the gate had thinned as the fate of each of the missing was revealed. The entire city seemed to quiet in collective grief.

Within days the media, being what it was, rallied the people together in anger over the horrendous affair. The public was crying out for blood, and the government was only too willing to comply. An investigation was launched. Someone's head would be served on a platter.

But through it all the desolate sound of a mournful sob kept playing through his mind. That coupled with a pair of somber brown eyes brought him back, time and again, to the woman he had held in his arms.

Was she planning to jump? Was that what the dream was telling him? He didn't know if it was a dream, anymore—it might all have been real. He had seen her in his waking hours. He had touched her on that plane. He knew it had to be her. No one else could be that beautiful. She was real. And she was in trouble.

As always, he would pull himself out of his reverie to confront the matter at hand. The embers were still smoldering, but he had to deal with all the legal and moral obligations of this tragedy. There was no time, he had to remind himself, to fantasize about the unknown.

Still, he had not slept in days, and he knew that sleep was the only way he would see her. She had proved to be elusive when he had scoured those mountains for her. Every lead had turned out to be a dead end and yet, he couldn't help but feel that he had been getting closer.

* * * *

Nida walked into the great room to find Del watching television and knitting. She was clucking her tongue at what was happening on the tube.

"What a shame," Del said as Nida entered. "All those people dead...Oh, dear, you don't know."

Nida stopped to stare at the picture. She recognized the skyline in the news report as that of her hometown. "What's happened?"

"A terrible fire—a factory owned by Cannan Enterprises just burnt to the ground. Sixteen people are lost."

Nida watched the scene. The fire had been put out, but there was nothing left. She had driven by that place many times. It employed more than 300 people. How horrible. She didn't believe she knew anyone that worked there but the catastrophe hit home, just the same. She could only imagine the suffering of the families left behind and that of those who would be unemployed this winter. It would be a blow to the entire city. She felt her own sadness deepen with this new tragedy.

A man was being interviewed, looking as though the entire world was weighing on his broad shoulders. His face, covered in soot and dirt, was a study of grief. He was telling of the people lost and those that would suffer financially for years. No one knew how the fire had started and an investigation was underway.

Nida watched intently as the man was interviewed. Or rather, she watched his expressive eyes. They were green and glittered like emeralds as he answered the reporter's questions. Nida had seen those eyes before, she was almost sure of it. His blackened face was impossible to see clearly but his eyes held her attention.

Later that evening, Del served Nida soup in front of a blazing fireplace. The night had grown chilly and damp while she stared into the flames as she toyed with her spoon.

"Honey," Del coaxed, "you have to eat. You'll never get your strength back if you don't."

"I'm sorry," was all she could say.

"You're thinking of those people that died in Chicago, ain't ya?"

"No, not exactly," Nida replied with a twinge of guilt. "I was thinking about someone I saw on the TV."

"That CEO they interviewed? He's a handsome critter."

Nida smiled in spite of herself. "He was that," she chimed, taking a sip of her soup. She barely tasted it as she concentrated on her thoughts. "Do you think it's possible, I mean really possible that this man in my dreams is a real person?"

"Why, sure. Stranger things have happened. I've seen wonders with my own eyes. Just because 'they' say it can't happen doesn't mean it can't. Why do you ask?"

"I'm not sure why but I have the feeling that he's out there and that he's looking for me."

"Could be. Now eat your soup. Eat every bite."

Nida complied mechanically, forcing the cooled liquid nourishment down. She hoped he would come to her at dawn, even if he wasn't real. She needed this fantasy to sustain her.

That night she dreamed of scorching green eyes and a warm, seeking mouth but when she woke at dawn, she was alone.

* * * *

Liam took his third shower of the evening, but he still couldn't get the smell of smoke and burning plastic off his skin. With a towel wrapped around his waist, he ambled into the sitting room of his hotel suite. He helped himself to a snifter of brandy and dropped heavily into an upholstered chair. A sudden desolation doused him with something near pain.

It shouldn't be like this. He shouldn't be alone. And she shouldn't be alone. He wondered if she had any knowledge of him. What if he was the only one of the two that was experiencing what was happening in his dreams? It suddenly occurred to him that he was thinking like a madman. Dreams, they were only dreams. How could anyone else know what was going on in his mind when he slept?

Liam gulped down a mouthful of the passable brandy. But she was real, he thought. He had seen her and touched her. Hell, he had even smelled her scent. And, he knew, something was wrong. He couldn't explain the rush of dread that came over him at that thought, or the connection he felt to her. Something had brought them together, and it had to be more than a passing fluke. There was a reason he was dreaming of her—a reason that they were together on that plane.

He guzzled the remainder of his nightcap and staggered to the bed, exhaustion driving him into a deep sleep filled with visions of her.

Chapter 7

"Ah, you're looking much better today, pet," Delma proclaimed. She set the laden tray across Nida's bedcovers and unfolded her napkin. Lifting the lid on the plate, she chided, "You will eat every bite if'n I have to feed you myself."

Onida did not feel hungry, but had found out it was best not to argue with the motherly nurse. Besides, she was learning to enjoy having someone take care of her.

"What was it like growing up in these mountains, Del?"

Delma's eyes took on a mystical light. "It was wonderful. There are no strangers up here. Everyone looks out for his neighbors. And there is solitude. Living up here means being alone without being lonely, if you can understand that. I would run and fish with my four brothers. The summers were barefoot and endless. If I close my eyes I can still smell my mother's blackberry cobbler calling us home.

"When I was little the whole world was right here in these hills. I couldn't have imagined anyplace better than this. Oh, we worked hard. It's a burdensome calling, scratching a living out of these mountains, but we never wanted for love." Del smiled at her fond memories. "I was lucky to go off to school. Pap saw to that. Told me someone with my inclinations should be a nurse, so that's what I did. And he was right too. But I hated to leave here; even those short years that I was gone. Came right back as soon as I could. I married a doctor and we raised our four kids up here. I was glad of that. I wanted my younguns to have that same life that I had. I expect they couldn't ask for better."

"Where are your kids now?"

"My two daughters're married. Margie, my youngest, is in Knoxville with her husband. They own a grocery together." Del's face beamed. "She's got one in the oven now, due early spring. My other girl, Joanie, is in Virginia. She has two babies and they run her ragged. Caleb is my oldest boy. He's a career man in the Army, got his captain's bars last year. But Georgie, I don't know what to do with that boy. He was always a dreamer. He wanders around the world finding new things to try. Why, last year he decided he wanted to fly planes. He's got his pilot's license and flies tourists around on sightseeing tours in California. Before that it was SCUBA diving for sunken treasure, and before that he was aiding famine victims somewhere in Africa." She clucked her tongue at the thought.

"I think Georgie is your favorite," Nida said with a knowing smile.

"Aw, I love all my kids just the same." Del was a bit embarrassed as she added, "Still, Georgie is a little special to me, I suppose. I'm proud of them all. I wish their father had lived to see how they turned out."

Nida couldn't help but feel the sadness that had crept into Del's eyes. It was a sadness born of a loss that she herself had experienced on far too many occasions.

Delma stared at some point in the distance and sighed. "After he passed and the kids all moved away, there didn't seem to be any reason to keep the house. Too many memories—made me sad. I sold it a few years back."

Nida swallowed her last bite. "I would imagine it can be difficult to live with so many happy memories and no one to share them with. So, you must have an apartment where you live in town?"

"Heavens no! Me? In a town? I just go where I'm needed. Mostly I live with folks who need tending, like now. Or I stay with my brother. He lost his wife a couple of years back. 'Course, sometimes I think he gets a little tired of me. There now," Del changed the subject as she cleared away the breakfast tray. She set it on the table near the door. "You know my life's story, now it's your turn."

"Not much to tell," Nida said as she tossed back the covers and put her feet on the floor.

"Baloney. Where were you born?"

"In a little farming community in western Illinois. My father had a farm and my mother was active in the local church."

"What else?"

"Well, um..." Nida didn't like to talk about herself or her history. It was difficult finding the words. She cinched a terry robe around her frame as she stalled for time. "I was fairly young when my parents died so I don't remember too much about growing up there."

"Oh, honey, I'm sorry. I didn't mean to pry." Del looked so repentant that Nida rushed to comfort her.

"No, it's okay. Really, I don't mind. I was eleven that year and the Bauer boy from across the road had given me my first kiss. He was thirteen and very cute." Nida had to smile at her own memory. "But the weather that summer was strange and especially unpredictable. A tornado landed on our farmhouse and my parents and my little brother were killed. I was at a sleep-over at a friend's so I was safe.

"After that I was sent to live with my father's mother in Springfield. After my parents' estate was sold and the debt settled, there wasn't much left. What there was, Grandma had put into a school fund for me, and she had to work to support us. That's when I started to write, I was alone so much."

It was Nida's turn to be saddened.

"The work was too much for her, I suppose. She died in her sleep when I was seventeen. I always felt responsible for that. After that I was sent to live with my mother's uncle near St. Louis. I never even knew Mom had an uncle. She never talked about him. That didn't work out so well. He was a bitter man, hateful and mean, all the time. When he tried to force me to sign over my college fund to him I got myself an attorney. I became emancipated. By the time I had gone to live with him I had completed a book of short stories. Shortly after I left his house I found an agent and got it published. Bobby loved the work as soon as he read it. He and his wife took me into their home. That's how I came to live in Chicago."

"He's a good man, your Bobby." Del left the room to draw water into the bathtub. Her heart was heavy with all the sadness Onida had suffered in her short life. She was more determined than ever to help her find happiness.

After a long soak in the tub, Nida joined Del downstairs. The great room was fragrant with aromas from the kitchen. She followed her nose and found her nurse hard at work over the stove.

"What is that heavenly smell?" Nida inquired.

"Those stories made me hungry for cobbler," Del answered with a giggle. "I found some frozen berries in your freezer. I just wish we had some homemade ice cream to plop on top of it."

For the first time in weeks Nida felt like eating. "Can I help?"

Del eyed her thoroughly. Nodding her head as if pleased with what she saw, she answered, "I think it will do you good. The cobbler will be done in about thirty minutes, and I thought we should have fish for lunch. Why don't you make the salad?"

Nida felt almost enthusiastic as she reached into a cabinet for a salad bowl. It seemed like a purely natural thing to be doing, preparing a meal with her new friend.

"Onida," Del recited the name as if exploring its sound. "What kind of name is that? It's very unusual."

"American Indian. My mother's mother was a Sioux, I believe. Mom told me once that after I was born they had gone to her family's home and had a naming ceremony for me. Onida means 'the one who is searched for' or something like that. I never really met any of her people. I think I would have liked to know them."

"Searched for...? Hmm."

Nida had to laugh at the tone in Del's voice, "Just what are you hatching?"

She had gotten to know this woman over the past weeks, and it seemed she was always brewing up some intrigue. She was amusing to watch—and contagious.

"Oh, nothing," the older woman said as she turned back to the skillet on the stove.

"Come on. Tell me what's on your mind."

"It's just that, well, you were telling me that this dream-man of yours is looking for you, or, at least, that's how you feel. Maybe it's fate that he finds you."

"Oh, come on! Even if this man was real, why would he be looking for me? He's just a figment of my over-active imagination." Still, Nida couldn't help but wonder.

Chapter 8

Liam felt as if he had been through a meat grinder. After six hours in meetings with OSHA and fire and arson investigators on Monday he was ready for a break. He found himself walking along the streets of Chicago, wandering aimlessly, waiting for the next round of meetings to begin.

He saw a corner hotdog stand and realized he hadn't taken time to eat since yesterday. He smelled the smoky links and his mouth began to water. Liam approached the window and ordered a Red-Hot with everything, just the way he liked it. The wiener came oozing in mustard and hot sauce, and dripping with onions and relish. Topping it off with a bag of potato chips and a cola, he was just sinking his teeth into the first savory bite when something in a store window caught his eye. He froze mid-bite, never noticing the relish and mustard that dribbled down the front of his coat.

It was her; the woman from his dreams was staring back at him from the display in the window in all her radiance. Her eyes danced with light and mirth, her luscious lips curved upward just slightly in a mysterious smile that seemed to promise anything a man could desire. Her long dark hair was loose and flowed about her shoulders in a jumble of curls.

Liam dropped his forgotten dinner and sprinted for the door of the shop. It was locked. The sign declared that the store had closed early due to illness. He scrambled to the window only to discover that with the lights in the store off, and the way the display was set up, he could not make out her name or even why her face graced the poster. Fury pounded through his soul as his fists hammered against the glass of the window.

His mind raced as he tried to make out the words on the sign by cupping his hands through the crossed slats of the security gate against the glass and peering in. It was no use. Liam pulled a small tablet of paper out of his breast pocket, writing down the address before studying the lay of the street. Checking the hours posted on the door again, noting that the little shop would not open again until nine a.m. the next day. Somewhere in the distance a clock chimed, and he realized that he had to get back to the state's attorney's offices. Glancing at his watch, Liam hailed a cab, watching the storefront from the back glass of the taxi until it disappeared from sight. He felt like he was a step closer to her and yet, still so far away.

* * * *

The air was thick with the scent of woodlands and morning dew, the stillness all around her seeming preternatural. Somewhere a mockingbird called out in the distance. The misty fog descended upon her balcony as it had done so many times before, but this was different. She knew he had come.

Onida slid off the bed and flew to the balcony doors, throwing the glass doors open to let the fog flow in around her feet. She breathed a sigh of relief as she felt his presence in the early morning gloom. She slipped into his arms as he stepped from the murkiness of the mist into the room, as he swooped her up and carried her to the bed. His longing kiss devoured her mind so completely that she had momentarily forgotten her resolve to confront this wraith in an effort to understand what was happening to her. She was disrobed as her body arched and quivered under his touch; somewhere in the smoky fog of her mind a voice told her to speak.

"Wait," she said as she weakly pushed against his shoulders. "Wait, I need to talk to you."

The man raised his head, looking at her with startling, dark green eyes that held the power to draw her in.

Nida licked her lips, not knowing what it was she had planned to say." I..." Her voiced trailed off as her arms wound around his neck and pulled him down for her kiss. He trailed his lips along her jaw line to her throat. "My name is Onida," she said against his ear just before she was lost to the moment.

She moaned as the morning mists swirled across the wooden floor unnoticed. The man in her arms was warm, alive and passionate. He had to be a real man, not a conjuring of her deep need.

His hands slipped under the small of her back, pulling her up against him. His seeking hardness found her, entered her with incredible, tender force. She cried out, wrapping her legs about his ribs to hold him to her. She found herself climbing higher and higher to the summit of that wonderful sensation that she had come to know so well.

His mouth swallowed her scream as she toppled over the edge. He raised up onto his arms then and quickened his pace, driving them both to the brink once again. She watched in amazement as he threw back his head and howled, grinding against her in intense joyful agony. She cried out again as she joined him in that soaring bliss.

They clasped one another in the graying light, exhausted and spent. Nida lay with her head on his chest. His flesh was warm. She could hear the beating of his heart, before rising up to look into his eyes. Studying his face, she imprinted every line of it on her memory. He was beautiful, and there was something in his eyes that spoke to her, an eerie waning emotion that she could not quite name.

His arms came round her, pulling her head down to rest against his chest again. It felt so perfect lying with him. She sighed softly and let her eyes close, happily fatigued, breathing in the fragrance that was the mysterious man beside her. They drifted together in the blissful contentedness that always followed their lovemaking.

* * * *

Liam awoke with a start, glancing at the unfamiliar surroundings of his temporary home. The stark corporate apartment left him feeling confused for a moment before the echoes of a voice came back into his memory. "My name is Onida."

She was trying to communicate. She was aware of him, was alive in the dream just as he was. This realization galvanized him into action. Tuesday had come and gone, and it had been impossible for him to seek out the store where he had seen her face. He would not miss another opportunity to find this woman. Liam threw back the covers and headed for the shower. Within twenty minutes he was dressed and flying out the front door of the apartment building.

He couldn't find a cab. The sun was still low in the sky, and he realized that most of the Windy City was still fast asleep. The chill of the morning air went unnoticed as he ran through the city streets while life began to stir around him. He would get to that damned store if he had to run every step of the way.

Finally spotting a taxi, he jumped out into the street and whistled sharply. The cab squealed to a stop for the well-dressed man, soon having him on his way to getting some answers. Again he went over in his mind the various complications of the situation. Her name was Onida, he had seen her on a plane in Tennessee, her picture was in a window in Chicago, and she was nowhere to be seen. If this step didn't hold any answers, he would hire a private investigator to find the woman.

In the dream she was still pale and thin, although she hadn't looked quite as ill as on the plane. Still he knew that something dark and dangerous was haunting her. He had to find her—needed to find her. He just plain needed her. This realization came as a shock to him. He had never needed anyone, as his two ex-wives were quick to point out.

"Driver," he ordered. "Go faster. I want to get there now."

The driver was not fazed. "Gonna cost ya, mister," was all he said as he pushed the gas pedal down a little farther.

"There's a hundred dollars in it if you get me there in less than five minutes."

Liam found himself propelled against the back of the seat as the cabby floored the battered old taxi. The car skidded and slid sideways. It landed directly in front of the little shop where the woman's picture was. The shop looked deserted.

"Coulda told ya it was closed at this hour. That'll be $122."

Liam fairly tossed the money at the driver as he exited the vehicle.

"You want I should wait for ya?"

When the fare didn't even glance at the driver, the cab sped off into the morning. Liam stepped up onto the curb, looking at his watch. Seeing that he had a two-hour wait before the store opened, he pulled out his cell phone to call his secretary. Meetings would have to be pushed back; his attorneys would be angry, but this had to be taken care of first so that he could focus on the day.

He paced and placed calls, rearranging schedules and talking to principal parties for an hour and a half before a man unbolted the folding gate across the front of the shop. Liam approached as the man opened the front door. He followed the clerk inside.

The clerk turned to speak. "I'm sorry. We don't open for thirty minutes yet."

Liam pushed past him and headed for the window display. He recognized the shop as being a bookstore. He snatched a book off the display and stared at the cover. Onida Burke, the name was imprinted on the cover in bold black ink. "What do you know about this author?" he demanded as he held the book up to the clerk.

"Uh, her work is quite popular," the man started.

Liam cut him off. "I want to know how to find her."

The sales clerk looked this man over. He was well-dressed and well-groomed—obviously a man of means. There was a determination about him and a gleam in his eyes that the clerk didn't care for. He was that uppity rich type that was used to giving orders.

Liam took another step toward the man, the clerk falling back a pace. "She's from here—Chicago, I mean. The name of her publisher is in the front of the book. She did a signing here a few weeks ago."

Liam pulled some money out of his wallet and slapped it down on the counter before exiting the bookshop, clutching the book against his coat.

Excitement was mounting somewhere in the region of his heart. He knew he was going to find her.

Chapter 9

Onida walked down the stairs, humming a little tune. It was a gorgeous day, she decided, and she was going to take a long walk, and maybe even do a little fishing. She hadn't fished since she was a child, and wondered if there was any tackle in the shed out back.

"You're certainly in a good mood this morning, young lady," Del said with a gleam in her eye.

"Yep, I feel pretty good today." Nida stretched her arms overhead and gave a big sigh as she landed on the main floor.

"You ought to, from the sounds I heard coming from that bedroom before dawn."

Onida was abashed. "I had another one of those dreams." She couldn't quite look Delma in the eye.

"That weren't no dream, honey."

Onida shot a glance at the old nurse. "What do you mean?"

"If it was a dream it woulda been only your voice I heard. Either there a bear in that room with you this morning or you had a man in your bed."

Onida was startled. "You mean you heard him?"

"He growls like an old bear. Passionate sort of fellow, ain't he?" Delma shot her a wink.

All thoughts of fishing fled as Nida wrapped her mind around the idea that there had been a witness to what she was experiencing in this cabin. If Delma had heard his impassioned sounds then that meant he had to be real. But how could that be? He appeared and disappeared with the fog. He never spoke words. He always seemed so otherworldly.

"I don't understand," Nida said as she sank to a sitting position on the bottom step, her minimal strength leaving her.

"Oh, dear, I've upset you." Delma Clack was all concern when she approached her young charge. "I hope I didn't spoil it for you. You were so happy a moment ago."

"No, Del, I'm all right." She patted the older woman's hand. "It's okay. It's more than okay. Do you know what this means? It means that you can hear him."

"Yes," Delma said as if speaking to a child. "I hear him."

"Don't you see? If you can hear him, you can see him. If you can see him he has to be real. He's not just a dream. This is all too weird."

* * * *

It never ceased to amaze Liam how quickly money could make people talk. The manager he spoke to was not forthcoming, but the young assistant editor was more than happy to tell him everything he knew for a quick hundred. Before 10:00 a.m. Liam was standing in the outer office of one Robert Goldman, Literary Agent, waiting to be admitted to his private office.

Liam was not accustomed to waiting. He paced restlessly while the sanctimonious secretary eyed him with disapproval. There was a buzz and she picked up the telephone receiver. Replacing it in the cradle she peered over her glasses at him. "You may go in now."

Liam fairly charged through the door that led to Goldman's inner office. He saw a small man who wore a ridiculous spotted bow tie. He took the smaller man's offered hand and introduced himself.

Goldman's face took on an expression of genuine concern as he began to speak. "So you're the Liam

Cannan. I'm truly sorry about the recent tragedy. It'll go hard on the entire city this winter."

"Thank you, Mr. Goldman," Liam replied impatiently.

"Bob, please. No need to stand on formality here."

"Bob," Liam began. "I'm looking for a client of yours. I would really appreciate it if you could get a message to her."

Bobby looked a little startled. "Well, I'll certainly try to help if I can. Who are you looking for?"

Liam held up the book he had purchased earlier that morning. "Onida Burke." He watched as the expression on the other man's face changed without warning.

"I'm afraid that Ms. Burke cannot be reached," he answered tersely. "She's out of the country at present."

Liam took a seat opposite Goldman and studied the man for some moments, trying to judge the reason for the sudden change before charging forward. "I have no wish to cause her harm, Bob. I know that she's not out of the country. She's somewhere in Appalachia, I believe."

Bobby looked startled again. "Why would you think that?" He wasn't at all sure he liked this young man.

"One reason is because I saw her getting off a plane in Knoxville a few weeks back..." Liam hesitated to name his other reasons.

"What is it you wish to see her about, Mr. Cannan?" Bobby's voice was all business now.

Liam absently plucked a piece of lint off his trousers. How could he explain the issue to this man without sounding insane? He decided to be as honest as possible. "Well, sir, I don't know how to explain it but I think she is trying to reach me."

"Oh?" Bobby thought for a moment before continuing. He leaned forward and folded his hands in front of him on the desk. "I have to tell you, Mr. Cannan, I consider Nida a member of my family. We are very close and she has never mentioned anything to me about attempting to get hold of the CEO of Cannan Enterprises."

Liam scratched his head. "You see, Mr. Goldman," he replied with a slightly embarrassed smile. "She may not know who I am. I only discovered her identity this morning."

Bobby was becoming more disturbed by the moment. He scrutinized the man closely. "If she doesn't know you then why would she be trying to reach you?"

"I know she's in trouble," Liam said, ignoring Goldman's question. "I think I'm can help her."

"What makes you think she's in trouble?"

"The last time I saw her she didn't look well. Something is eating her alive. I think you know that as well as I."

Bobby's eyebrows shot up. "What do you mean, 'the last time'? Do you see her often?" If there was a new love-interest in Nida's life he damn sure wanted to know about it.

Liam made a show of checking his watch. He had no way of answering that without looking like a madman. "Look, I have to be in a meeting in less than thirty minutes." He opened Nida's book to see her picture on the inside of the book jacket. Taking a pen out of his pocket he scribbled something on the inside cover, closed the book and handed it to Goldman. "If you could just give this to her I would really appreciate it. I really need to talk to her; and she with me." Liam stood and offered his hand to the agent.

Bobby stood to shake the man's hand. He watched Liam exit then returned to his seat. He thought for a moment over the strange meeting with the CEO and chief stockholder of Cannan Enterprises. Looking down he saw the brand new copy of "The Broken Promise," Nida's latest work of mystery fiction. He flipped the cover open to read the cryptic words written by the strange man. His eyebrows shot up again as he read them aloud.

Bobby closed the book and slipped it into his desk drawer. Poor Nida had enough to worry about without adding a lovesick fan to the mix. He decided to wait until she was stronger again and then make up his mind whether he should give it to her.

Chapter 10

Several days had gone by and Nida still had not seen her mysterious lover since Del had admitted to hearing him. She had been feeling stronger under her nurse's watchful care. She was thinking about work again, and trying to decide if it was time to head back to the Windy City.

With phone in hand, she sat at the kitchen table to dial Bobby's private cell phone. She felt just a touch of homesickness when Bobby answered with his usual business-like tone. "Hi, Bobby. How's it going?"

His tone abruptly changed. "Nida! Sweetheart, it's good to hear your voice. You sound much better. How are you feeling?"

"I'm doing a lot better, thanks. You were right. I needed a break. But now I think I might be ready to get back to work."

"Well, there's no hurry to jump back into it. I told Randall that your manuscript won't be ready until after the first of the year due to illness, and he said that would be no problem. They'll still gladly publish it. You're good as gold to them."

Onida hesitated as she decided whether she should tell him what was on her mind. Finally she charged headlong into the subject. "I was thinking that I would put that one away for awhile, Bobby. Before you go off half-cocked, let me tell you what I was thinking."

She heard Bobby take a deep patient breath before responding. "Okay, tell me what you got."

"Well, I'm thinking of doing another kind of mystery this time, something besides the usual murder crap that I'm always cranking out. You see, I have this idea about a strange romance. It's kind of like a haunting. The heroine lives up here in the mountains and has visions about a man that comes out of the mists at night during every full moon. He just sort of appears. She falls in love with him but doesn't know who he is or even what he is, but he becomes her reality. What do you think?"

Something in what she said struck a note with Bobby. He pulled open his desk drawer and flipped open the book that Cannan had left with him. Mists and reality, he thought. "Bobby, are you still there?" asked an uncertain Nida.

"Yes, honey, I'm still here. What made you come up with that idea?"

"I don't know," she lied. She didn't want to have to explain too much. "It just sort of came to me while I was watching the moon the other night."

"I need to ask you something. Do you know a Liam Cannan?"

Nida thought for a moment. "No, should I?"

"No, I was just wondering."

"Wait, isn't he the guy that owns that place that burned down up there? What a tragedy."

"Yes, he is. Nida, you know I will never tell you what you should write about. If you have that story in you, then you should write it. If you're asking how I think it will be received, the only answer I can give is I just don't know. The readers have come to expect a certain type of story from you."

"Well, maybe it's time we hit a whole new group of readers. Anyway, I think I'll go ahead and do it. And, Bobby, if you don't mind, I think I will stay here for awhile longer. I kinda like being around Delma. You done good when you picked her, old boy."

"I'm glad you liked her. I think I interviewed a dozen different people before I found her. I thought you could use a little mothering."

Onida felt her throat tighten slightly as his words brought back memories of her mother. "You did well, Bob. Thanks. You know where to reach me if you need me, and make sure someone checks my apartment every so often, will ya?"

"I've been doing that myself, once a week. All is well."

"Thanks again and take care. Oh, and say hello to Doreen for me. Del is teaching me to knit. I'm making her an afghan but don't tell her. I'll give it to her at Christmas."

Bobby smiled. It was good to hear his girl's enthusiasm starting to return. "I'll give her your love. You just enjoy yourself and call if you need anything."

"I will. Love you."

When the call ended, Bobby removed the book from the desk drawer and read the hand-written words again. "Out of the mountain mists and into reality." What could it mean? He replaced the book and slammed the drawer shut. He decided that he needed to have a word with the nurse, see if she could shed any light on what was happening.

* * * *

Liam looked at his watch again, and then checked his cell for messages one more time. Why had she not called? As he dressed for the day's round of meetings he decided to pay the little literary agent another visit. He wanted to be sure that Onida Burke had gotten his message.

It would be time to return to the East Coast again soon, and he had to know what was going on before then. There was an ache in his loins as he thought of the beautiful author. There was also an ache in his chest. Uncertainty had been clouding his judgment of late, and he decided that enough was enough. He would force the man to tell him where she was, if he had to choke the little twerp with his own bow tie.

He left the small apartment, tucking his cell phone into his coat pocket. He just had to know if she was all right. He had to know.

Chapter 11

It was nearly 5:00 and Bobby had sent his faithful secretary home early. The weather was turning ugly and he wanted her to get home safely. As he gathered his own things to head for home, the door to his office burst open.

"I think you and I need to talk," a very determined and wind-blown Liam Cannan nearly yelled at him.

"If you don't mind, Mr. Cannan, I was just about to head home. It's late and the weather is getting pretty bad." Bobby was more than a little startled by the man's sudden appearance.

"But I do mind, Mr. Goldman. Did you give Onida my message?"

To Bobby, Liam looked like a man possessed. His clothing was rain-spattered and disheveled. His rumpled hair was plastered wetly about his face and the wild expression in his eyes didn't help matters. "No, I didn't."

Liam felt a measure of rage building deep inside. "Why the hell not?"

"Mr. Cannan," Bobby said with a sigh. "To be honest, I just don't think it would be appropriate to bother Ms. Burke at this point in time. She is recuperating from an illness and doesn't need to be upset or confused right now."

Liam's expression changed. "I knew it. How is she? Will she recover?"

"It's nothing too serious. She just needs rest. Now, if you don't mind..."

"Mr. Goldman, I need to see her and I believe she needs to see me. You can either help me or I will find her on my own."

Bobby set down his briefcase and took a seat. "I can appreciate that you think you need to see her but without knowing any of the particulars I simply will not risk my client's well-being. Please understand. She's like a daughter to me."

Liam relaxed slightly. "I don't wish to cause her any stress. I think that I can take some of that stress away. Please. Talk to her. I'm sure she will want to see me."

"Mr. Cannan, I already spoke to her. She says she doesn't know you. I'm sorry."

"You gave her my message?" Liam was bewildered. He was just sure she would recognize the meaning of his words.

"I asked her if she knew you, she said no."

Leaning forward, Liam put his palms on the man's desk. He glared at him, trying to control his temper. "Give her my message. She will know what it means."

"I'll do what I can, Mr. Cannan."

"I'm not leaving here until I have your word."

Bobby stared up at Cannan. He could tell that this deranged person was not likely to give up. "I will send the book to her in the morning. Will that suffice?"

Liam removed his hands and stood straight. "I would appreciate that. I'll be waiting for your call to tell me it's done." With that he left the office.

Something in Goldman's eyes, Liam decided as he boarded the elevator, told him that he was lying. He knew the call would never come. When the lift reached the ground floor he fished his cell phone out of his pocket and placed a call. He would have to take matters into his own hands. When Mary answered at the other end, he told her to find him a private investigator. He had to find Onida Burke. He wouldn't rest until he did.

* * * *

"How nice to hear from you, Mr. Goldman," Delma Clack said after answering the phone. "Nida will be sorry she missed you. It's a beautiful morning here. She decided to go out walking. You wouldn't believe how well she's doing."

"Well, um, Mrs. Clack, it's you I wanted to talk to. You two getting on well?"

"Why, sure, that girl is just a love. I do believe that we're getting to be right good friends."

"Good to hear. I was hoping you could shed some light on what's going on with her. Has she been seeing anyone?" He thought again about the strange man that had been glaring at him just the night before. How could his Nida be involved with such a person?

"No, I don't think so. We haven't had any visitors, unless you count that worthless Hiram Jones that brings us our supplies. I swear I don't know why she puts up with a drunk like that..."

"You're sure that she's not?"

"What's this all about? Is something wrong?"

"No, I just wanted to check."

"Don't lie to me. I can hear it in your voice. Best you fess up right now. I need to know if there's gonna be trouble."

"Mrs. Clack," Bobby said uncertainly.

"You call me Del like everyone else, y'hear?"

"Okay, I don't know how to say this but there's been a man looking for her. I don't know what to make of this guy, but he seems hell-bent to find her."

"Who is this fella?" Delma was more than a little concerned.

"He's actually a man with a pretty high profile. One of his businesses burned a few weeks back and there's an on-going investigation. I'm afraid that the stress may have left him a bit unhinged."

"You talking about that terrible fire in Chicago?" Delma clucked her tongue. "That was a shame, all those people dead. Nida and I watched it on the satellite. What was that fella's name again?"

"Liam Cannan."

"Oh, yes. He's a good-looking cuss. Why would he be looking for our girl?"

"I think he saw her picture in a bookstore display or something and has become obsessed with her. He gave me a message, written in a copy of her latest novel. He wants me to send it to her." Bobby opened the book and began reading the inscription, "Out of the mountain mists and into reality..."

"Uh oh," Delma interrupted him.

"What is it?"

"Now, Mr. Goldman, I don't want you to worry about a thing. I want you to send that book right out, you hear me?"

"What's going on?" Bobby demanded.

"I think the less you know about this the better off you'll be. Just send it out right now. It's important and that's all you need to know."

"I'm not sending this unless I know what's happening."

"Don't be a fool. If you care at all for that girl, you'll send that book. Now, I don't have time to argue anymore. I can see Nida coming up the path so I have to hang up. You do as I say or I'll come over there and tie into you, y'hear?"

Bobby looked at the dead receiver. The woman had actually hung up on him. He wondered who she thought she was, talking to him in such a manner. Still, he found himself handing the novel and a short note to his secretary, requesting that she send it to Nida via over-night express.

* * * *

"How was your walk, honey?" Delma looked with pride at her young charge. She had color in her skin and she was starting to fill out a bit.

"It was wonderful. You know what I just realized? Tomorrow is Halloween."

"They'll be a dance in town tomorrow night, would you wanna go?" Delma chimed hopefully.

"I don't know," Onida smiled. "Maybe. Will you go if I do?"

"Are you kidding me? Bobbing for apples and blind man's bluff—I never miss it. Looks like we'll be needing some costumes. I'll get right on it. I'll bet we could come up with something around here."

"I'll give you a hand. Sounds like fun." Nida followed her nurse up the stairs to begin looking through the closets and cupboards.

"Some say that All Hallows Eve is the day that the wall between this world and the next is thinnest. If'n there are spirits about this will be the night that they come to find us. Lots of superstitions in these here mountains. Some of the folk up here..."

Delma's conversation faded as Nida thought about the mysterious man from the mists. He had not been back in some time. She woke every morning before dawn hoping to see him, but he was nowhere. Maybe, if the mountain tales were true, she would finally get to see him again. And maybe this time he wouldn't disappear...

She mentally shook herself. He was just a fabrication of her troubled mind. But somewhere deep inside was a loneliness that only he had been able to fill. There was sadness growing in her as she realized that she had been trying to believe in an illusion. But then she remembered that Del had heard his voice. How was that possible?

Chapter 12

Liam dozed as the Cessna Citation aircraft carried him out of Chicago's Midway Airport. It had seemed to take forever to get clearance to take off. The aircraft's other seven passenger seats were empty. It was rare for him to take a flight without at least some members of his staff on board.

He had arrived at the airport before daylight that morning, being unable to sleep. Onida Burke had become foremost in his mind. Even at that moment, as he closed his eyes and leaned his head back against the leather seat, her pale face drifted into his mind's eye.

Dawn had not yet broken the horizon as the aircraft's landing gear left the runway. The rumbling of the plane's jet engines faded away as he drifted into that moment of time between awake and asleep. Her face drifted closer. He could see the hope in her eyes as she turned to see him.

* * * *

Onida woke as the first gray light of dawn filled her bedroom. This had become her habit. She had left the balcony doors cracked open in hope that her mysterious lover would find his way to her again.

A mockingbird trilled out his song. Nida felt a prickle of excitement at the sound. The fragrance of the morning forest filled her room as the mist rolled in around the opening in the door. Did she dare to hope?

Sliding off the bed Onida listened to the bird. It seemed to call to her, drawing her to the balcony. She padded softly through the distorted environment of her room to those doors that would, hopefully, lead her into his arms. Her body tingled as she placed a shaking hand on the door to pull it open.

His form, silhouetted in the haze of the gray mist, was only a few feet away from her. She released her breath in a rush as he spread his arms in invitation. In just a few moments she would be lost with him in that rapturous world that they had created together.

Onida stepped forward and watched in bewilderment as the mists seemed to grow around him and swallow him. She ran forward but he had disappeared.

Nida cried out at her despair. She dropped to her knees and buried her face in her hands. The mockingbird had ceased his winsome song.

Then she heard a voice. It was deep and rich and masculine. "I'm coming, Nida. I'll be there, just hold on."

* * * *

Liam lifted his head with a start as turbulence shook the small aircraft. "Damn!" he roared as he punched the armrest of his seat. He had just been moments away from taking her in his arms again. He had seen the pain in her eyes as he was torn away from her. It mirrored the pain in his heart.

He absently rubbed his chest as he peered out the window into the darkness. Soon, he told himself. There was an envelope on the table in front of him. It contained the address of the elusive Onida Burke, as discovered by the private detective whom his secretary, Mary had hired. It hadn't taken the investigator long to find Nida and for that Liam was grateful. He would never know peace until he could see her—for real—in the light of day or the dark of night, but for real.

He fingered the envelope. He went over everything in his mind again. The rental car had been ordered. A map with the directions to Wakanda Mountain plotted out was in his coat pocket, and a copy of The Broken

Promise lay open in front of him. He looked at her picture on the book jacket again.

"I'm coming, Nida," he said to the photograph. "I'll be there, just hold on."

* * * *

As Halloween day wore on, Nida wondered if she should tell Del what she thought she had heard early that morning. They worked together on their costumes for the coming dance. Delma had made arrangements for the Bensons, one of Onida's neighbors to give them a ride into town that night.

Somehow, after what had happened that morning, Onida no longer felt like going to the party. Her spirits had taken a brutal blow. She tried to put on a good face for Del. The woman was so looking forward to some entertainment. Onida had decided that she would go, if only for the nurse's sake.

"Okay, that's the tenth sigh. What's ailing you, girl?"

Onida, jolted from her dismal thoughts, looked up from the shimmering fabric in her lap. She offered a smile she didn't feel. "Nothing, I'm just a little tired I guess."

"I see. Well," Del stood up, holding out the outfit she had been stitching together, "my costume's finished."

Nida giggled in spite of her mood as she looked at the clown outfit that Del would be wearing to the dance that night. "You're a wonder, Del. Give you a few scraps of cloth and you whip up a masterpiece."

She looked again at the fabric in her lap that would be her costume for the night. Del had managed to find one of Nida's old dresses, left behind on a previous summer visit, and enough odds and ends to piece together an outfit that could only be described as celestial.

Delma picked up the gossamer layers of cloth from Nida's lap. "You're gonna look like a fairy princess in this get-up. You'll be the prettiest one there, I'd bet my eye teeth." Del heard Onida sigh again. "That's it. Time you and me took a walk. You need fresh air."

Del pulled Nida out of her chair and dragged her into the bright afternoon sunshine. As they disappeared into the lush forest, they didn't see the delivery truck that drove up the long lane that led to the house, or the delivery man who got out carrying a package.

Standing on the expansive front porch of the cabin, the deliveryman knocked several times. Finally determining that no one was at home, he checked the instructions on the delivery invoice. No acceptance signature was required, so he propped the package against the front door.

Chapter 13

Liam's hands began to ache before he realized how hard he was gripping the steering wheel. He loosened his grasp and forced himself to relax. The sun was beginning to set.

He cursed McGhee Tyson Airport, all its employees, the car rental company, his pilot and the city of Knoxville, in that order. Heavy air traffic had forced his pilot to remain in a holding pattern for an extra hour before they were allowed to land.

When they had finally touched down and Liam was able to make his way to the rental counter, they had cancelled his reservation due to some clerical error. Two rental companies and three arguments later, he had managed to acquire the nondescript gray sedan that was careening down the road.

Halloween traffic in the city of Knoxville and the surrounding communities had been insane. He thought that he would never get to the open roadways. A deep sense of desperation was causing him to ignore the warning voice in his head as he crushed the accelerator down a little harder.

* * * *

Onida looked as if she had just arrived from some magical realm. She surveyed her costumed body in the mirror. The elfin creature that gazed back at her should have filled her with excitement for the night ahead. She used to love Halloween and all its traditions, but memories and ghosts haunted her unmercifully. She sighed and turned away from the mirror.

"Nida," Delma called from the hallway. "Are you ready? The Bensons are here. We better get a move-on."

Onida walked out of her room. At the bottom of the stairs she grabbed her wrap and headed for the front door. Turning to her companion behind her, she gave her what she hoped was an enthusiastic smile.

As the door opened under her hand, she spied the Bensons' vehicle parked in front of the cabin. The family of four waved eagerly at her as she pulled the door open wider. Something landed on her foot with a thump. Her eyes wandered downward to see what it was. It was a small package. They hadn't seen that when they returned to the house after their walk; they had come in by the kitchen door.

"I see that agent of yours is capable of doing what he's told," Delma quipped. She reached down to retrieve the box.

"This is from Bobby?" Onida accepted the parcel from her friend. "I wonder what he sent me."

"Well, it's not from Bob. He called yesterday saying that someone had given it to him. I told him to forward it on at once. Looks like he knows what's good for him. You're going to want to open that now, Nida. I think it's what you've been searching for." She stepped past Onida into the darkness of the evening. "I'm going with the Bensons. If you want to join us later you just call the town hall and I'll send someone out to fetch you. But something tells me you won't be joining us. Have a good evening and don't wait up." Delma walked down the steps and to the waiting car.

Onida watched as the vehicle's taillights disappeared down the tree-lined lane. She stepped back to close the door, looking at the package in her hand. Walking to the kitchen she dug a knife out of the drawer and sliced through the binding tape. Inside the box, amid the packing peanuts, she found a copy of her latest novel and a hand-written note from Bobby.

Nida,

A very strange man brought this book to me, insisting that I forward it to you immediately. After speaking to your over-bearing nurse I was persuaded to send it on. I look forward to your explanation of the inscription inside the front cover.

Yours,

Bob

A frown furrowed Nida's brow. She set the note aside and removed the book from the box. Butterflies were tickling the pit of her stomach as she smoothed her hand over the cover. She had a sudden thought that whatever lay inside would change her life forever. She was afraid to face it.

Steeling herself and taking a deep breath, she slid her thumb under the bottom corner of the cover. Slowly, as if fearing that something evil would fly out of the book, she opened it. She looked at the words, written in a tidy hand, and tried to comprehend what they said. Her addled mind told her to read the words aloud. "Out of the mountain mists and into reality. I'm here for you. Please call me. Liam Cannan, 312–555–

1919." Hearing the words brought a lump to her throat. Could it be?

Her knees felt weak, her feet staggering to the kitchen table where she sank into a chair. Holding the book in her shaking hands, she read the words again. Was this Liam the man from the mists? She closed her eyes and took a deep steadying breath. Unbidden memories of his body cloaked in the shadows of the pre-dawn fog raced into her mind. A shiver of pure pleasure dashed up her spine. She could almost feel his lips touching the tender flesh at the base of her throat, and his warm arms pulling her body close to his. Another shiver trailed over her and she opened her eyes again.

Onida pounced at the cordless telephone hanging on the wall. She made three tries at punching in the digits of his phone number before she finally got it right. By the fourth ring she realized she was holding her breath.

She exhaled as voice mail answered the call. The greeting, recorded in the man's own voice, was little more than a request to leave a detailed message. She sat for a moment after the beep, not knowing what to say or how to say it, finally disconnecting the call.

She paced across the kitchen and out the side door. The evening air was turning crisp, and a gentle breeze stirred the tree branches overhead. Breathing deeply, she used the air to brace her jagged nerves. She still had the phone in her hand as she walked along the path that led to the front of the cabin.

Somewhere in the distance a mockingbird called out into the darkness. The butterflies in her stomach increased their frantic dance. The dampness around her ankles began to grow heavier. Looking down she could see an early fog rolling across the path.

Onida accelerated her steps as she rounded the corner of her house, something catching her attention through the woods. She stopped to crane her neck and finally caught a glimpse of it again. Through the trees in the direction of the road was a red light winking through the gathering mist.

She dashed through the front door of the cabin and found a flashlight, dropping the phone on the table near the door as she exited again. Armed with her light Onida tromped through the trees in her fairy costume toward the blinking light. She was sure it was a car, but something in the way it was sitting didn't look normal, as if it was possibly off the road. She wondered if there had been a wreck.

Onida reached the vehicle at last; it was a gray sedan, sitting at an angle off the road with the front end sticking up out of a ditch. The driver's door was hanging open. The mountain mist rolling across the ground was making it nearly impossible to discern which direction the victim must have taken.

Nida decided, as she tramped back through the woods toward home, it would be best to call for help. Once she reached her front porch she stopped short. What the hell is going on here?

Chapter 14

Nida distinctly remembered having closed the door, yet here it was standing half-open. The mockingbird's song grew louder. She turned back to look along the lane as the misty fog swelled, curling through the trees and up the lane, sweeping toward her and the cabin. The night took on a preternatural quality that made her feel as if she had just moved into another plane of existence.

She stepped forward, pushed the door open a little farther. Peering into the entranceway she saw nothing amiss. She put first one foot and then the other into the swirling mists that had wandered through the open door, slowly moving toward the center of the great room. Nothing seemed out of the ordinary except the ghostly fog that crawled over the floors as she peered into surrounding rooms.

At the bottom of the staircase, she looked upward until she was certain that nothing was changed about the stairway. Then she heard a noise. It was just a small noise, barely heard over the song of the mockingbird that hovered nearby. It had come from upstairs. She dashed up the stairway, taking the steps two at a time.

The minute her feet touched the top floor, she felt that presence. Her heart quickened. How could this be? It was early in the evening. Dawn was hours away, but she sensed him just the same.

Onida wasted little time in thought. She was scarcely breathing as she fairly flew through her bedroom door. The lamp that she had turned off earlier was glaring brightly. Looking around she saw the balcony doors were open. The growing lump in her throat threatened to choke her, and her heart hammered so hard against her ribs that she experienced real pain.

Each silent step she took toward her balcony only seemed to force it farther away. She was afraid that she would never reach it. Finally she stepped through the doors and into the thickening mountain fog.

Glancing around, she didn't see anything, or rather, anyone. Disappointment was already climbing in her breast before something at the far corner rail caught her attention. She took a step closer and could see the vague outline of a man. Her heart skipped a beat and the lump in her throat nearly exploded.

As she took another step, she could just make out that the man was bent forward, gripping the railing with his head hanging down over his chest. His posture was so forlorn. Onida wished to touch him, to drive away the sad incline of his shoulders as she took another step closer.

The man's body suddenly tensed. He returned to his full height with his head up straight. It was impossible for her not to recognize his tall, powerful form. She knew him, even from behind, but there was something different about him. The difference wasn't just that he was wearing clothes, either. He didn't seem so much a part of the mist now. It was hard to put her finger on it but he was different.

The man turned slowly to face her. Standing in the fog as he was she could barely make out his features, but she could feel the intensity of his gaze. He took the first step in her direction, and she felt her breath catch in her chest. Dizziness washed over her, causing her to fall back a step.

He took another stride toward her. He was coming out of the shadows and into the light of her bedroom. Closer still he moved until she could see how green his eyes were. His hair was dark and curling in the dampness. It looked real, not softened and dreamlike.

His face was rugged, handsome, and she could see a small bleeding cut above his left eyebrow. His shoulders were broad and strong.

His eyes never left her face as he stepped ever closer. He was close enough now to reach out and touch. Onida opened her mouth to speak but nothing came out. She took another breath. Her tongue darted across her lips as she prepared to try again.

"Are you real?"

Liam had to strain to hear her words, so soft was her voice. He took another step to close the distance between them. His vision drank in every detail, from the way her eyes beseeched him, to the way the mist and the light played around her shimmering costume, giving her an ethereal quality. To him she looked like an angel and it had nothing to do with the flowing white garment she was wearing.

He reached up a hand to brush his knuckles along the line of her cheek. He saw her eyes close briefly as he touched her. When she looked up again he told her, "Yes, I'm real."

Onida let a tiny whimper escape her lips. Her body was tense, feeling as rigid as a statue. His hand on her face felt so good and so warm, but she didn't think she could trust herself to know reality. "Liam?" she asked tentatively.

A small smile tugged at the corner of his lips. "Yes," he whispered. "You got my message?"

"Liam," she said the name a little louder. Hearing her own voice speak it seemed to make him a little more corporeal. Her body had come alive with sensation with every nuance of the night flowing over her at once—the night song of the bird nearby, Liam's breath on her skin, his fingers lightly stroking her face, even the heat of his nearness filled her senses. His scent was the same, redolent of fresh air and timberlands.

"Onida," he breathed her name out. "You're a witch who has captured me. You've haunted my life. You fill my dreams, and when I wake alone I feel empty."

She breathed out a little moan. "I didn't...I thought I made you up. But you're real."

"Yes," he said, flattening his palm against her face. His other arm slowly wrapped around her back and pulled her against his warmth. He touched the top of her head with his lips. "Onida, I thought I was dreaming again when I first saw you a moment ago. Onida."

A wrenching sob tore from her throat. She clutched the front of his coat and tried to get her breath. She leaned her head back, her lips parted. Her eyes pulled him down, beckoned to him as her arms moved upward to encircle his neck.

Not even the heady mountain night could compare to the searing power of that first passionate kiss. The staggering intensity shut out everything but the two of them drawing together in a physical collision of the senses. There was no balcony, no mockingbird. The mist, the trees, the world itself was lost in this moment that these two souls had for so long searched.

As their kiss deepened, Liam's arms crushed her more firmly against his body. Nothing in all those dreamlike experiences had prepared him for the all-consuming power of her waking touch. It was only the need for life-sustaining oxygen that forced their lips apart.

Both were deeply shaken as they clung to one another, gasping for breath. He buried his face in the curls that cascaded over shoulders, inhaling her fragrance, breathing her essence. This was so much different than being the dreaming marionette that was driven to take her as he slept. This was his own free will finally taking charge. He could savor every moment in her arms. He would know her heart and her mind. He would make love to the whole of the woman and not just her body.

"Liam," she breathed against his chest. "Tell me you won't disappear into the fog. Please say you'll stay."

There was a note to her voice—hopeful and yet desperate—that tugged at his soul, causing fierce emotion to render him momentarily speechless. He tried to pull her closer, to absorb her into his own body.

He was shaking, and he could feel those same tremors vibrating through her body. He pulled his head up to look at her again. With his finger hooked under her chin he guided her face upward, willing her to look at him. She had tears in her eyes and an expression of profound fear. He wanted to wipe that fear away. He desperately needed to see her eyes sparkle with joy. He never wanted to see those haunted shadows cross her vision again.

He lowered his lips to hers again in a throbbing, tender kiss. A sob caught in her throat as a moan rolled out. Her body melded to his. She was opening herself completely, offering herself to him. Liam reluctantly released her mouth, his eyes searching hers. "I'll never leave you as long as you want me."

Nida threw her arms around his neck, jumping upward with a joyful cry. He lifted her from her feet and held her tightly as her legs dangled in open space. He needed to see her in full light, having had enough of shadows and mists.

He carried her into the bedroom before setting her on her feet again. He held her away from him, filling his vision with the sight of her. The tears that had been shimmering in her eyes had overflowed onto her pale cheeks to trickle down to her sunny smile. He took her face in his hands and smoothed away the tears with his thumbs.

"My dreams have come true," he said as he pressed his forehead down against hers. "I'm touching you, I'm holding you. I never thought I'd find you."

She pressed one of her hands against his; her other hand held onto his coat. She struggled to get her mind around how the apparition that came out of the mists in the gray light of the hazy mountain dawn was a real man, and that he was standing in her room, holding her, talking to her.

It was completely natural to hold this stranger, to touch him and kiss him. She could feel the connection of their souls, for it was their souls that had brought them together.

She leaned her head back again, touching his lips with hers. His hands held her face still, and his lips parted to let his tongue tease her mouth open. As she opened to him, she felt his hands move to the back of her head, and then travel downward over her neck, tracing the curve of her back. The thin fabric of her dress only served to enhance the erotic feel of his fingers pressing into her flesh.

Onida whimpered softly into his mouth. The kiss ended as his lips went searching for more pleasure. He found the sensitive pulse at her temple and wandered lower to her throat. She gripped his shoulders for fear that she would fall into a great abyss and lose him forever.

Liam tore his mouth away from her smooth skin. He wanted to look upon her again, to feast on her with his eyes. He studied every curve of face, etching the way she looked at that moment into his memory. As long as he lived he would always remember her as she was right then.

He took her hands in his and kissed the tips of her fingers. "I have never felt this kind of need for anyone."

He released her hands then, and ran his fingers up her bare arms. When his touch came into contact with the silky fabric of her gown at the top, he slipped his fingers under the straps. He watched her eyes as he guided the cloth off her shoulders and down her arms. He let the flowing garment slide slowly into a pool on the floor.

Taking a step back, he let his gaze feast on the banquet of her beauty as he shrugged out of his overcoat. Her lush curves were far more sensual than his dreams had revealed. Her breasts, clad in the sheer lace of her bra, were round and full and proud. The curve of her hip begged to be caressed. Her lace panties did little to hide her feminine secrets, and those were secrets he wanted to know.

In his shirtsleeves, he stepped forward to take her into his arms again. His hands explored her flesh at will as his mouth descended for another kiss. Her naked skin felt like hot silk under his touch.

He was awed by the amount of passion she returned. When their lips parted, they were both panting. He kissed her again, letting his lips trail over her jaw and down to the smooth skin of her shoulder.

Her fingers began to work at the buttons on his shirt, moaning at the touch of his lips on her bare skin. His fingers reached behind her, unhooking her bra. Onida released his shirt long enough to let the straps fall from her arms. She returned to the task of getting to his nude skin. She was desperate to feel his hot, real flesh against hers.

Liam raised his head and took his hands off her body only long enough to assist her. Both their hands were shaking as they struggled with the little buttons. Finally, Liam tore the offending garment open in frustration. The buttons plinked as they bounced across the room, but he already had his shirt off and was sucking air between his teeth at the sensation of her hands and lips against his chest.

Nida reveled in the salty flavor of his skin as she nibbled. She ran her hands over his muscular frame, thrilled and exhilarated by his body. She heard him gasp as her teeth grazed one of his nipples.

With his hand he turned her face up to his again. He took her sweet mouth in another kiss to stop her exploration. He was in danger of losing control under her seeking mouth and hands.

He fanned his fingers out over her shoulders and dropped to his knees. He let his hands follow him down her body, grazing her drawn nipples as his mouth found her soft belly. His wandering fingers found the waistband of her silky underpants and skimmed the skin underneath.

Onida's labored breathing matched his own as he pulled his mouth from her sweet flesh long enough to slide the undergarment slowly down her legs. He lifted each foot in turn, removing her shoes and slipping the panties away from her skin. Her warm sexual fragrance bewitched his senses.

His lips skimmed over her ribcage as he slowly rose to his feet. Liam's vision drank in her naked form; a body that promised eternal joy to the man who captured her heart. With the tips of his fingers, he brushed a stray lock of hair from her face. "I'm in love with you," he whispered, his voice ragged and raw with emotion.

Fresh tears flooded into Onida's eyes as she captured his caressing hand and pressed it against her cheek. Her smile told him everything he needed to know as he lowered his mouth to hers again. Her arms went round his waist, clinging to him in desperate need.

Pulling back slightly, she looked up into his green eyes. "I can't believe you're here," she said as she took his hand. She led him to the side of her bed and stood in front of him. Her soft hand skimmed over his chest as she reached up to touch his throat and his face. The growth of whiskers felt coarse against her palm. His nearness, his redolence, the warmth of his skin had stoked a burning fire that was spreading rapidly through her limbs. "I dared to dream that this moment could happen. I hoped that you could be here, touching me, holding me."

He growled her name as his arms crushed her to him. Shaking with need he seized her mouth in another burning kiss, more demanding than the last. He sank with her, lowering her down onto the mattress and releasing her long enough for his fumbling hands to unfasten his trousers and drop them to the floor. He kicked in frustration to remove his stubborn shoes and fell onto the bed to tear his socks from his feet.

Onida's arms opened as he turned to her. Soft mewling sounds escaped her parted lips as his mouth found the flesh at the base of her throat and moved lower to the satiny skin of her breasts. She arched against his mouth as he suckled her nipple. With fingers tangled in his hair, she held him to her and moaned out his name.

It took all his will to keep from losing control at her eager response to his touch. He wanted to plow into her, to bury his aching shaft to the hilt in her flesh, but a deeper need forced him to hold himself in check. He desperately needed to hear her cry out in pleasure. He wanted to feel her body explode against his. He needed to know that part of the dream was real.

He moved to her other breast as his fingers toyed with the dampened nipple that his mouth had just released. He felt her fingernails bite into his scalp as her body wriggled beneath him. Her moans were sweet torment. He struggled against his ever-increasing feral need for release.

Onida brought her knees up around him, dragging her feet along his legs. His mouth and hands, the feel of his body pressed against her, and his warm breath stroking her skin were working together to drive her mad. Her mind was no longer capable of rational thought as he drove her pleasure higher. She moaned at the loss of his tongue and fingers on her breasts. He moved lower, nipping at the sensitive flesh of her ribs, and lower still to her belly. His hands captured her writhing hips as his exploring tongue found her navel.

"Liam," she gasped. "I can't take any more."

He answered her with a moan as his mouth moved lower. He raised his head and looked at what her parted legs revealed to him. His fingers touched the soft, tender skin there, wrenching another moan from her throat. He was thrilled to find her wet to his touch as he gently stretched the drenched folds of skin open with the fingers of one hand while the other stroked the exposed inner flesh.

Onida's voice cried out as his thumb came into contact with the hidden, swollen ball of nerves. He softly, slowly massaged the hard knot, watching the rapture on her face. Her legs opened farther as her hips moved under his stroking fingers.

He inhaled her pure erotic perfume and slid one finger into her soaking flesh. She gasped, her body becoming even more animated. Her pelvis pumped against his fingers as she voiced her pleasure in guttural tones.

He pushed a second finger into her and lowered his lips onto the hard ball of nerves. He heard her scream as he took it into his mouth, flicking at it with his tongue. He stroked her inner flesh with his fingers in a constant, unrelenting rhythm. Her bottom barely touched the mattress as she pressed her hips upward into his face. The higher her pleasure climbed the more difficult it became for him to maintain control.

Her voice suddenly became silent as her body tensed. He felt her womanly inner muscles clench around his fingers. Then a moan started deep in her chest to emerge from her mouth as a cry. Her body convulsed at the onslaught of the orgasm that overtook her. He drove her onward with his mouth, with his fingers, drawing the pleasure out for as long as she could take it.

He released her pulsing clitoris as she crashed against the mattress. He marveled at the way she clenched in spasms around his fingers.

"I want to feel you inside me," she begged.

His self-control shattered under the husky resonance of her voice. He had never encountered anything as powerful as her unbridled sensuality. He drew his knees up under himself and took hold of her hips. With one mighty lunge, he buried himself in the silky heat of her flesh.

He pulled himself out almost immediately and drove back into her. Falling forward onto his outstretched arms, he drove into her again and again galvanized by her sounds of pleasure.

Onida's hips met his every thrust with equal abandon. Her nails dug furrows across his back and down his arms. Sparkling pinpoints of light shattered in her vision. She cried his name as the tightening coil deep within her loosed its energy in a tremendous explosion.

Liam pounded into her furiously as her muscles seized and clenched around his member. His primal growl echoed through the room as he erupted inside her. With each lunge he filled her womb with his seed. When finally their shared climax receded, he collapsed on top of her and buried his face in the fragrant hair that surrounded her head.

Nida brought her leaden arms up around his neck. Her fingers absently stroked his hair as her body shuddered and quivered. "Are we still alive," she whispered in a panting breath.

He raised his head slowly. He looked into her eyes before dipping down to place a gentle kiss on her trembling lips. He gave her a smile full of emotion. "I'm not sure."

She giggled softly as her arms tightened around his neck. He scooped her into his arms and rolled onto his back, taking her with him and dislodging his manhood. She curled up against him. With her ear pressed against his chest she could hear the powerful thump of his heartbeat. She prayed that this was not just another extraordinary dream.

At some point in the night Delma Clack returned home. As she walked past Nida's bedroom, she glanced in to see two figures snuggled together under the glow of artificial light. Warmth filled her soul for the girl whose heart had been so badly broken. She sighed and quietly stepped forward to pull the bedroom door shut.

The dream-lovers had found each other at long last.

Chapter 15

As the first rays of chilly dawn filtered in through the open balcony doors, Liam began to stir on the bed. His hand unconsciously reached for her. When he discovered the other side of the bed to be empty, his eyes flew open. He sat up and glanced around the strangely familiar room.

He saw her. She looked like a goddess standing in the golden light of the sunrise at the open door. Her hair was tousled and her eyes were sparkling. She was wrapped in a quilt that hid her delicious body from view.

Relief washed over him as he smiled at her. "What are you doing over there?"

"I couldn't sleep. I was afraid if I closed my eyes you would disappear again."

He stood and walked to her. His arms wrapped around her shivering body. "But I'm still here. We're both still here."

Nida nuzzled her face against his hard chest. She sighed at the joy she felt against his body. "Liam, I love you."

He suddenly pushed her away from him. His hands reached to cup her face. Their eyes locked as he searched for some sign that he had heard wrong. Finally he lifted her wrapped body and took her back to bed.

He worked the quilt away from her skin as his lips found hers. He lifted his head to look into her dark eyes again. He placed her feather-soft hand against his chest. "You've lived in here for so long. I've always loved you. Now that I found you I never want to live without you again."

Nida's breath caught in her throat. All the pain and emptiness of the past months—of her entire lonely life—disappeared as his heart pounded against her palm. A happiness she never dared to hope for filled her soul at that moment, and she gave herself over to it gratefully.

"Just try to get rid of me," she rasped out.

Her hand moved up to stroke his unshaven jaw. Her lips accepted his kiss and returned it ardently. His arms went round her and pressed her against his heat. She felt his arousal push against her belly, sending quivering sensation to the center of her being. She moaned against his lips as he rolled onto his back and pulled her on top of him. His stroking fingers traveled the length of her back to cup her bottom and drag her against his growing shaft.

Onida's hips rocked against him as her lips moved to his neck and chest. She wanted to explore the body that had given her such pleasure. The sound of his breath becoming ragged was like music to her ears as she continued to discover all the places he liked to have touched.

His lips spoke her name more than once as she moved along his torso, licking and nipping her way down. She discovered his nipples were sensitive to her mouth, as was the skin under his ribcage. As she moved lower, her breasts brushed his cock and he moaned loudly. She rocked her shoulders slightly, rubbing her flesh back and forth over his hard erection.

His hands grasped her shoulders as his pelvis lifted against her erotic caresses. She raised her head to look into his cloudy eyes before continuing her southward route. Her nails grazed the outline of his pelvic bone as her tongue traced a path from his navel to his groin.

His fingers tangled in her hair as her hand closed around his hard cock. She kissed the tip and ran her tongue around the tender edge of the head. His body tensed. His breath rushed out in a snarling moan. "My God, Onida..." he growled.

She ran her tongue over the length of his hardness, feeling it throb and pulse under her touch. Her lips wrapped around the head as her tongue massaged the silken tip. She tasted the salty drops of fluid that it released uncontrollably. She pushed her mouth slowly down, taking in as much as she could.

Liam's feral growl was the only warning she had before he grabbed her away from his pulsating manhood. He pulled her roughly up his body and dragged her legs apart to straddle his hips. His fingers reached behind and under her, finding her open and ready. She leaned forward and arched her back, pushing her wetness onto his probing hands.

"I have to be inside you," he moaned as he stroked her opening. He clutched his cock and positioned it at her entrance. She pushed downward as he drove up into her. His fingers took hold of her hips and held her motionless. They stared into each other's lustful eyes for long moments as he twitched and throbbed inside her.

Liam slowly lifted her hips, sending ripples of sensation through her. Nida dug her nails into his chest as her body gradually slid down the length of him. He filled her completely only to lift her again. She moaned into the still morning air and slipped downward, inching along his mass until she was full again.

She moaned a ragged breath as she lifted her body. His hips rose to meet her as she slowly lowered herself. She had never known such pleasure as this man's body was giving her. Not even the chilly morning air could penetrate the world that their bodies created.

She could hear Liam's harsh breath rattling in his chest. It was a purely lustful sound that delighted her. She continued her deliberate pace, fascinated by the feel of his hardness moving slowly within her. She watched his eyes. She had never given herself so openly to any man, and this man was giving just as much of himself.

Liam moved a hand off her hip and across her soft belly. He splayed his fingers over her skin as his thumb hooked under her pelvic bone, seeking her clitoris. She cried out sharply at the first touch against her most sensitive spot.

He worked his thumb in slow, deliberate circles over the hardened center. She shuddered and threw her head back. Her response caused the aching in his cock to intensify. He moved under her, forcing the pace to accelerate. She leaned back with her hands planted beside his thighs. She pressed her feet flat against the mattress and pumped wildly against him.

Their moans mingled together in a sensual chorus. He could feel her inner muscles tightening around his shaft, and knew she was close to coming. He released her clit and grasped her hips. He thrust into her in quick, powerful strokes, driving them both to the edge of reality.

Onida screamed his name as her back arched until her long hair touched his legs. He plunged into her again, clutching her hips and pressing her pelvis against his in a grinding motion.

Sweet, hot fluid jetted into her as the spiraling waves of climax caused her insides to clench. He rammed into her again, growling like a wild animal as he shuddered under her. A combined flood of liquid flowed from her onto his groin. He drove into her one more time, holding tightly, forcing himself in as far as he could go.

As the last waves of his orgasm shook him, Liam momentarily lost control of his muscles, releasing her hips. Nida fell back against his legs, shuddering and gasping. His cock still throbbed within her, a truly wondrous sensation.

After a few moments Liam's hands stroked up along her inner thighs. He brushed his knuckles across her exposed clit, and was rewarded by her shiver. "Making love to you is like a walk in paradise," he whispered hoarsely.

Onida reached her hand out to him. He gripped it and pulled her upright. She was grinning at him when her face came back into view. She leaned down and kissed his lips before falling over next to him in a languid heap. "The sun is up and you're still here," she said as she laid her head on his shoulder. "I can't believe this is happening. Wait 'til Del meets you. She's going to be thrilled."

Liam's hand idly stroked her shoulder. "Who's Del?"

"She's my friend. She was hired to take care of me after I got sick. She's the only one I ever told about you, even suggested that you might actually be a real person." She stopped for a moment before continuing. "I think she knew that we would find each other."

Liam rolled her over onto her back and settled over the top of her. "I thought I was losing my mind when I first started having those dreams. I thought it was the stress of my business troubles that was causing me to conjure your image.

"Then, a few weeks ago I saw you. I caught you as you almost fell when you were getting off the plane in Knoxville. I didn't actually see your face until you walked away from me and I had to fight my way off the plane to try to catch you. I was too late and you were gone.

"I had to track you down after that. I couldn't rest or focus on anything but finding you. I was driven by something that I can't explain. Now that I found you and see that you know me as I know you, I'm never going to be more than an arm's reach away from you again."

Onida's heart fluttered wildly. "I was told that this cabin, this mountain was magical. I guess the tale was true because you're here and I love you."

They kissed again, long and passionately. Somewhere in the distance a mockingbird trilled his lovely song. Onida let herself believe that the wind in the waking trees sighed with contentment as Wakanda Mountain held the two lovers in her welcoming embrace.

They fell asleep wrapped in each other's arms, knowing that they would have the rest of their lives to love one another and bless the Appalachian spell that had brought them together.

The End

ABOUT MOLLY WENS

Known as SweetWitch by many readers, Molly Wens weaves spells of passion and romance in her writing. Her characters leap off the page and become a part of your world as they explore the forces at work in their lives. Sometimes gritty, often sensuous and always riveting, her stories are born of her fertile imagination and remarkable life experiences.

Molly has been writing for much of her life, starting at the tender age of eleven when she won her first national award in a school-sponsored essay contest. Her love of the written word has never wavered, and she has continued to win prizes and accolades for the many short stories she has in print.

Now living in the Midwest with her family, Molly can often be found reading, working, playing with her child and even jumping from the occasional airplane. Shelter from the Storm is the first of what we hope to be many commercially published novels by Molly Wens.

Web Site: www.mollywens.com

If you enjoyed <u>SPELL OF APPALACHIA</u>, you might also enjoy:

SHELTER FROM THE STORM
By Molly Wens

Life can change in the blink of an eye as Carissa James discovers while on an ill-fated business trip. Kidnapped, injured and left to her own wits in the frozen wilderness of the Grand Teton Mountains, she battles the elements for survival with nothing more than a spiritual guide, a white wolf, to see her through.

Bryce Matheny, though, knows all too well what can happen when the Fates play games with the lives of mortals. One moment on a dark highway and his beloved wife is gone. Left scarred and embittered, ostracized by society as a branded killer, he leaves the world behind, retreats to a mountain hideaway where he intends to live out the rest of his years, alone.

Another dark night changes Bryce's life forever when the howl of a wolf and the insistence of his faithful dog drag him from the safety of his cabin into the raging winter storm. That's when he finds Carissa, half-dead, buried in the snow.

Afraid she will see him as a monster, he tries to hide his disfigured face. When he finally allows her to see, he is struck by the pure desire in her eyes. He wants to share that desire with her, but wonders if it still lives within him as he watches her scantily clad body reclining on his bed.

Passion wins and love is born, but the moment cannot last. She has no choice but to return to her children and her home.

For Bryce, life without Clarissa is sheer torture. Haunted by the memory of her soft caresses and fiery green eyes, he becomes a man possessed. But does he have the strength to face his past and go in search of her? Will his damaged soul once again find her to be his shelter from the storm?

Warning: This title contains graphic language and sex.

REVIEWS FOR SHELTER FROM THE STORM

Stacy Link, Paranormal Reviews

Molly Wens draws her readers into Carissa and Bryce's lives and has you wanting to see them come together. The reader will enjoy how Bryce cares for Carissa and how Carissa works to heal Bryce and bring him back to the world he left behind.

Dawn D, Manic Readers Review - 5/5 STARS!

I loved this book! It was well written, with incredible characterization, and an exciting plot. The sex sizzled and the romance would make anyone want a mountain man of their own. I highly recommend this story to anyone who loves romance.

Excerpt From SHELTER FROM THE STORM:

"All done," she said brightly. "That wasn't so bad, was it?" Standing back to see her handy-work she was struck by the pure manly beauty of him that caused butterflies to stir in her belly.

He watched her face as she appraised him, seeing his own burning hunger reflected in her eyes. Feeling with his fingers, he discovered just how close she had cropped his facial hair. There was not much left. The question of whether she would still find him desirable if she could see the damning scars played over and over in his mind until he found himself handing her the antique razor from the box.

"Finish it," he said, meeting her gaze directly.

She smiled brightly, but the smile soon gave way to a worried frown. "Um, are you sure you want me to do this? I've never wielded one of these things, you know."

"I trust you," he answered, his voice soft and husky.

Digging the strop out of the bottom of the box of toiletries, she hooked it on the back of his chair, dragging the blade of the razor repeatedly along the length of it. Bryce cringed inwardly with each metallic sound of the cutting edge being sharpened. Something akin to an icy fist seemed to be clenching around his heart, tightening with each passing moment.

Letting out a small giggle she brushed the lather over his beard in increments until all the black hair was covered. Carissa took a deep breath then pushed his face slightly to the side before dragging the blade down his right cheek.

As she moved to wipe the spent shavings onto a towel, he tried to think of something to distract his mind from his ragged nerves. "So, how did you learn to cook so well on a wood burner?" he asked by way of making conversation.

"Don't talk or you'll end up with a nasty gash," she admonished, stopping to sharpen the blade again.

He held up his hands in a half-hearted attempt to play the game, but waiting for her to discover what was hidden under the remaining hair on his face was nerve-wracking at best. He had no way of knowing at that point Carissa had found what she saw so far to be very much to her liking, or that she was daydreaming about being kissed by the sensual lips that were now visible. The only thing he knew was the fear that she would be repulsed by the destroyed left side of his face. He took another deep breath, anticipating the disgust he would see in her eyes, or worse, pity.

"You're going to have to hold very still. This side is a bit rough and I don't want to nick you," she warned softly as she laid the blade to his skin.

Carissa continued in silence until the job was done. Cleaning the remains of the lather away with a damp towel, she stood back to look. What she saw took her breath away and turned her insides gooey. She thought that if she had met this man under different circumstances he would already be parking his boots under her bed.

He had a strong, square jaw and a full sensual mouth that she knew had to have the ability to kiss her witless. There was a narrow scar that ran from the left corner of his mouth up to the hollow of his cheek where it spread out in all directions in a pattern similar to a spider web. Somehow the scar only added to the masculine nature of his face, making him all the more appealing to her eyes. A shudder of pure heat shot through her body, bringing a pink flush to her face, as she stood silently taking in the sight of him.

Bryce caught her shudder, disappointment bringing his hope down as he misinterpreted her reaction. Unable to look at her, unwilling to see the aversion he knew would show on her face, he closed his eyes. This would be the end of it, the hope, the dreams of her in his arms, everything.

"Damn, boy," Carissa fairly purred. "You're a hunk. You've done the women of this world a huge disservice by hiding yourself up here."

When Bryce opened his eyes it was to see the naked desire that burned in the immeasurable depths of her olive-green eyes. He knew instantly that what he saw could not possibly be an act, so raw was the visible emotion. She was so near that he could reach out and seize her, take her into his arms and crush her to his body; all he had to do was reach...

Bryce was on his feet in an instant, grasping her soft arms, pulling her into his embrace, descending upon her mouth in a voracious kiss. His lips worked over hers, feeling her mouth open softly, welcoming him unconditionally. The sound of her impassioned moan set his blood to boiling as his body shook with a need that nearly over-powered them both.

His tongue invaded, seeking and finding hers to entwine in a dance as frenzied as the wind that howled outside. Finally, he was forced to release her lips as the need for oxygen had them both panting. She was clutching his shirt, gasping and leaning heavily into him, her lips trembling as her little pink tongue darted out to taste the essence of the kiss that had so affected them both. He captured her mouth again, sucking on that delicious little morsel, unable to get his fill.

He came up for air a second time, struggling to regain control of his unruly need. "Cari," he rasped against her forehead. "If you want me to stop, tell me now. I don't think I can control myself much longer."

Carissa tilted her head back, reaching up, pulling his face down to hers. "Control is over-rated. I want you, Bryce. Make love to me." Her voice, throaty and soft, was a plea, begging him to take her, to make her his. "If you stop now, I may never recover."

BUY THIS AND MORE TITLES AT
www.eXcessica.com

welcome to
eXcessica

sweet
hot
forbidden

eXcessica's **BLOG**
www.excessica.com/blog

eXcessica's **YAHOO GROUP**
groups.yahoo.com/group/eXcessica/

**Check out both for updates about eXcessica books,
as well as chances to win free E-Books!**